Stories of

DOGS
WE LOVE

Stories of

DOGS
WE LOVE

Sixteen tales of unforgettable canine companions

SWEETWATER
PRESS

SWEETWATER
PRESS

Stories of Dogs We Love

Copyright © 2007 by Cliff Road Books, Inc.

Produced by arrangement with Sweetwater Press

ISBN-13: 978-1-58173-675-5
ISBN-10: 1-58173-675-4

Cover design by Pat Covert
Book design by Holly Smith

Table of Contents

Memoirs of a Yellow Dog
O. Henry

I don't suppose it will knock any of you people off your perch to read a contribution from an animal. Mr. Kipling and a good many others have demonstrated the fact that animals can express themselves in remunerative English, and no magazine goes to press nowadays without an animal story in it, except the old-style monthlies that are still running pictures of Bryan and the Mont Pelée horror.

But you needn't look for any stuck-up literature in my piece, such as Bearoo, the bear, and Snakoo, the snake, and Tammanoo, the tiger, talk in the jungle books. A yellow dog that's spent most of his life in a cheap New York flat, sleeping in a corner on an old sateen underskirt (the one she spilled port wine on at the Lady Longshoremen's banquet), mustn't be expected to perform any tricks with the art of speech.

I was born a yellow pup; date, locality, pedigree, and weight unknown. The first thing I can recollect, an old woman had me in a basket at Broadway and Twenty-third trying to sell me to a fat lady. Old Mother Hubbard was boosting me to beat the band as a genuine Pomeranian-Hambletonian-Red-Irish-Cochin-China-Stoke-Pogis fox terrier. The fat lady chased a V around among the samples of gros grain flannelette in her shopping bag till she cornered it, and gave up. From that moment I was a pet—a mamma's own wootsey squidlums. Say, gentle reader, did you ever have a 200-pound woman breathing a flavour of Camembert cheese and Peau d'Espagne pick you up and wallop her nose all over you, remarking all the time in an Emma Eames tone of voice: "Oh, oo's um oodlum, doodlum, woodlum, toodlum, bitsy-witsy skoodlums?"

From a pedigreed yellow pup I grew up to be an anonymous yellow cur looking like a cross between an Angora cat and a box of lemons. But my mistress never tumbled. She thought that the two primeval pups that Noah chased into the ark were but a collateral branch of my ancestors. It took two policemen to keep her from entering me at the Madison Square Garden for the Siberian bloodhound prize.

I'll tell you about that flat. The house was the ordinary thing in New York, paved with Parian marble in the entrance hall and cobblestones above the first floor. Our flat was three—well, not flights—climbs up. My mistress rented it unfurnished, and put in the regular things—1903 antique unholstered parlour set, oil chromo of geishas in a Harlem tea house, rubber plant and husband.

By Sirius! there was a biped I felt sorry for. He was a little man with sandy hair and whiskers a good deal like mine. Henpecked?— well, toucans and flamingoes and pelicans all had their bills in him. He wiped the dishes and listened to my mistress tell about the cheap, ragged things the lady with the squirrel-skin coat on the second floor hung out on her line to dry. And every evening while she was getting supper she made him take me out on the end of a string for a walk.

If men knew how women pass the time when they are alone they'd never marry. Laura Lean Jibbey, peanut brittle, a little almond cream on the neck muscles, dishes unwashed, half an hour's talk with the iceman, reading a package of old letters, a couple of pickles and two bottles of malt extract, one hour peeking through a hole in the window shade into the flat across the air-shaft—that's about all there is to it. Twenty minutes before time for him to come home from work she straightens up the house, fixes her rat so it won't show, and gets out a lot of sewing for a ten-minute bluff.

I led a dog's life in that flat. Most all day I lay there in my corner watching that fat woman kill time. I slept sometimes and had pipe dreams about being out chasing cats into basements and growling at old ladies with black mittens, as a dog was intended to do. Then she would pounce upon me with a lot of that drivelling poodle palaver and kiss me on the nose—but what could I do? A dog can't chew cloves.

I began to feel sorry for Hubby, dog my cats if I didn't. We looked so much alike that people noticed it when we went out; so we shook the streets that Morgan's cab drives down, and took to climbing the piles of last December's snow on the streets where cheap people live.

One evening when we were thus promenading, and I was trying to look like a prize St. Bernard, and the old man was trying to look like he wouldn't have murdered the first organ-grinder he heard play Mendelssohn's wedding-march, I looked up at him and said, in my way:

"What are you looking so sour about, you oakum trimmed lobster? She don't kiss you. You don't have to sit on her lap and listen to talk that would make the book of a musical comedy sound like the maxims of Epictetus. You ought to be thankful you're not a dog. Brace up, Benedick, and bid the blues begone."

The matrimonial mishap looked down at me with almost canine intelligence in his face.

"Why, doggie," says he, "good doggie. You almost look like you could speak. What is it, doggie—Cats?"

Cats! Could speak!

But, of course, he couldn't understand. Humans were denied the speech of animals. The only common ground of communication upon which dogs and men can get together is in fiction.

In the flat across the hall from us lived a lady with a black-and-tan terrier. Her husband strung it and took it out every evening, but he always came home cheerful and whistling. One day I touched noses with the black-and-tan in the hall, and I struck him for an elucidation.

"See, here, Wiggle-and-Skip," I says, "you know that it ain't the nature of a real man to play dry nurse to a dog in public. I never saw one leashed to a bow-wow yet that didn't look like he'd like to lick every other man that looked at him. But your boss comes in every day as perky and set up as an amateur prestidigitator doing the egg trick. How does he do it? Don't tell me he likes it."

"Him?" says the black-and-tan. "Why, he uses Nature's Own Remedy. He gets spifflicated. At first when we go out he's as shy as the man on the steamer who would rather play pedro when they make 'em all jackpots. By the time we've been in eight saloons he don't care whether the thing on the end of his line is a dog or a catfish. I've lost two inches of my tail trying to sidestep those swinging doors."

The pointer I got from that terrier—vaudeville please copy—set me to thinking.

One evening about 6 o'clock my mistress ordered him to get busy and do the ozone act for Lovey. I have concealed it until now, but that is what she called me. The black-and-tan was called "Tweetness." I consider that I have the bulge on him as far as you could chase a rabbit. Still "Lovey" is something of a nomenclatural tin can on the tail of one's self respect.

At a quiet place on a safe street I tightened the line of my custodian in front of an attractive, refined saloon. I made a dead-ahead scramble for the doors, whining like a dog in the press despatches that lets the family know that little Alice is bogged while gathering lilies in the brook.

"Why, darn my eyes," says the old man, with a grin; "darn my eyes if the saffron-coloured son of a seltzer lemonade ain't asking me in to take a drink. Lemme see—how long's it been since I saved shoe leather by keeping one foot on the foot-rest? I believe I'll—"

I knew I had him. Hot Scotches he took, sitting at a table. For an hour he kept the Campbells coming. I sat by his side rapping for the waiter with my tail, and eating free lunch such as mamma in her flat never equalled with her homemade truck bought at a delicatessen store eight minutes before papa comes home.

When the products of Scotland were all exhausted except the rye bread the old man unwound me from the table leg and played me outside like a fisherman plays a salmon. Out there he took off my collar and threw it into the street.

"Poor doggie," says he; "good doggie. She shan't kiss you any more. 'S a darned shame. Good doggie, go away and get run over by a street car and be happy."

I refused to leave. I leaped and frisked around the old man's legs happy as a pug on a rug.

"You old flea-headed woodchuck-chaser," I said to him—"you moon-baying, rabbit-pointing, egg-stealing old beagle, can't you see that I don't want to leave you? Can't you see that we're both Pups in the Wood and the missis is the cruel uncle after you with the dish towel and me with the flea liniment and a pink bow to tie on my tail. Why not cut that all out and be pards forever more?"

Maybe you'll say he didn't understand—maybe he didn't. But he kind of got a grip on the Hot Scotches, and stood still for a minute, thinking.

11

"Doggie," says he, finally, "we don't live more than a dozen lives on this earth, and very few of us live to be more than 300. If I ever see that flat any more I'm a flat, and if you do you're flatter; and that's no flattery. I'm offering 60 to 1 that Westward Ho wins out by the length of a dachshund."

There was no string, but I frolicked along with my master to the Twenty-third street ferry. And the cats on the route saw reason to give thanks that prehensile claws had been given them.

On the Jersey side my master said to a stranger who stood eating a currant bun:

"Me and my doggie, we are bound for the Rocky Mountains."

But what pleased me most was when my old man pulled both of my ears until I howled, and said:

"You common, monkey-headed, rat-tailed, sulphur-coloured son of a door mat, do you know what I'm going to call you?"

I thought of "Lovey," and I whined dolefully.

"I'm going to call you 'Pete,'" says my master; and if I'd had five tails I couldn't have done enough wagging to do justice to the occasion.

Christmas in a Brown Paper Wrapper
Ruth Beaumont Cook

I have no idea what made me stop and take a look at that crumpled grocery sack," said my friend. "It could just as easily have been somebody's garbage."

The sack was indeed considered garbage by whoever tossed it there, right in the middle of Shades Crest Road, on a cold December morning in 1976. Shirley parked her car on the shoulder, not far from the old fire surveillance tower that kept watch over Jones Valley. When she stepped into the road, she realized the sack was moving and almost backed away, but the faint yipping sounds from inside drew her hands and her heart. When she stooped down and carefully unfolded the sack, she discovered five tiny, mostly black puppies with their eyes barely open. They were wriggling all over each other.

"They're very young," said the Bluff Park veterinarian on Valley Street when Shirley hurried in with her discovery. "You might not be able to save them, but you can certainly try if you want to."

By the next afternoon, when I stopped by, Shirley was heartbroken. One by one, all of the puppies had died except the smallest female. "She's a feisty one, though," Shirley told me. "Come and see. She'll gulp down every drop of formula whenever I bring that eye dropper near her mouth."

Shirley led me to her laundry room and pulled back the pink terry towel she'd wrapped around the lone surviving puppy. Immediately, the tiny black puff began wriggling and yipping. "Wait here," she said. "I'll go get that dropper."

I reached down into the cardboard box, and the puppy immediately latched onto my little finger with a powerful sucking reflex. Barely open, her shiny black bead eyes were looking directly at me, and I wondered why she'd had the stuff to survive when her four bigger brothers and sisters had not. I also wondered what kind of lazy coward would drop a sack full of newborn puppies in the middle of a road for someone else to run over.

"Are you going to keep her?" I asked when we sat down to coffee. We'd moved the cardboard box next to the kitchen table, and the puppy had dozed off with a visibly contented tummy.

"I'd love to, but I just can't. We already have two dogs, and those spoiled little matriarchs won't tolerate her. I've had to keep them closed up in my bedroom ever since I brought those puppies home. Besides, we just don't need another dog."

I didn't say anything right then, but that evening, I talked it over with my husband. Our six-year-old had been begging for a puppy. He'd asked Santa a week earlier, but he'd also asked for Rock'em Sock'em Robots, so we'd thought perhaps we could put off the puppy until his birthday in May when housebreaking would be easier—newspapers and trips outside and all of that.

I called Shirley the next morning and offered to adopt. The catch was that she'd have to keep the puppy until we returned from Ohio right after Christmas the following week. Shirley agreed, and I set about composing a riddle that would explain how Santa had known to deliver Bobby's Christmas to Shirley's house. I copied the riddle into a card and wrapped the card in a big box with lots of Santa paper. Our older son Roger was already at the age of Santa Claus skepticism, so we kept the secret from him, too.

When we headed up the highway two days before Christmas, I was a little concerned that Bobby hadn't mentioned his puppy desire all week. Robots, yes. Puppy, no. What if he no longer wanted a dog? But that was ridiculous. What little boy didn't want a dog? I hoped it would be okay that she was a she. It certainly was with me. In fact, it would be rather nice to have another female in the house.

I had stopped by to see Shirley the afternoon before we left and was amazed at the changes in the puppy. Those jet black eyes were wide open now, and the little thing had learned to prop herself up on her hind legs and paw at the side of her box whenever anyone came near. Her yips were slightly more deep-throated, and there were now golden markings in her black fur.

"I think she's doubled in size just this week," said Shirley. "Look at those feet. They're almost as big as the rest of her."

"Did the vet speculate on what kind of dog she might be?"

"No, he said it was too early."

Well, I thought, time would tell. A little boy and his big dog. That image was fine with me.

Up through Tennessee we drove, then Kentucky, then across the river at Cincinnati, continuing our habit of leaving at six o'clock in the evening so the boys would fall asleep after an hour or two, thereby limiting the repetitions of "Are we there yet?". We would deposit them with their eager grandparents and fall into bed for a few hours the next morning after our twelve-hour drive.

I will never forget the gradually widening realization in Bobby's eyes on Christmas morning as his brother helped him open his package and read the riddle while we sat around the tree at my parents' home in Chesterland, Ohio. "A dog!" he cried. "It's a dog!" He couldn't wait to get home.

We named her Ginger for the color of her fur, which was definitely shifting from black by the time we returned to Alabama. My mental image of a little boy and his big dog turned out to be prophetic. Ginger grew and grew—and grew some more until the vet on Valley Street concluded that she was probably part German Shepherd and part Great Dane. Years later my son would say, "She was bigger than me, and that made her so much fun. She could always outrun me, even when I was older."

Bobby's first memories of Ginger are of bottle feeding her next to the cardboard box we moved to our kitchen when we returned from Ohio. Over the years, more and more memories piled up. One year we planned a scavenger hunt for Roger's birthday and attached the final clues to Ginger's collar so that his friends had to chase her all over the yard and wrestle her to the ground to get their clues. She, of course, loved every minute of it.

Ginger was a happy dog, except when the garbage truck entered our neighborhood. Her only antagonists were the two men who tiptoed down our driveway to empty the garbage cans. She'd begin barking and revving up her ferocity as soon as she heard their truck turn on to Mountain Branch Drive from Tyler Road. By the time they reached the back of our house, she would be in a frenzy—week in and week out.

Finally one morning, my husband had had enough. He stood up angrily from the breakfast table and stormed down the deck steps. The two garbage collectors, who were used to Ginger's tirades, were halfway up the driveway when Clayton summoned them back and suggested it was time for a truce. "If she gets to know you, she'll stop all that," he said with confidence.

"I don't think so, sir," said one of them, shaking his head. Both men flatly refused to pet the snarling Ginger, even through the fence, so the morning garbage can frenzy continued for years.

When she was nine years old, Ginger proved once again that she had the stuff to survive against great odds. I stepped onto the back deck one morning to check her water bowl and sensed something different. When I looked more closely, I saw that the whole right side of her head drooped crazily and that she was standing at an odd angle. Ginger cuddled up against me, and I could tell she was as puzzled by her condition as I was.

"I'm not sure exactly what it is," said the faithful vet on Valley Street. "Sometimes big dogs have strokes, just like humans." He suggested sending Ginger down to Auburn University for an evaluation.

We considered this, but a friend suggested we get a second opinion first, so off we went to another vet in Homewood. Though he was also not sure, he believed her condition involved muscle deterioration and suggested Cortisone as the first treatment option.

The Cortisone worked. It stopped the progression and restored all of Ginger's muscle tone except for the most severely affected area, which was her head. "She will never regain the use of those muscles around her right eye, but other muscles will compensate," the vet explained. As time went on, the only visible vestige was an odd bump on the right side of Ginger's head where bones were in place, but the muscle had sunk away.

Ginger was fine with this fate. She continued to jump up on her long legs and poke her head over the top of the backyard fence when anyone other than the garbage collectors approached the back yard. Her long pink tongue would loll from the right side of her mouth while she panted and waited to be petted. She was just as good as ever at snuggling with the boys on the couch while they watched television, at romping through piles of fall leaves, and also at industriously digging up any spring plants I tried to set out in the backyard—as if I'd put them there specifically for her to play with.

When she was fourteen, Ginger developed hip dysplasia, a joint deterioration disease. In dog years, she was almost a centenarian, so the vet explained that this was not unusual. By then, Bobby and his brother were adults—boys who had grown all the way up, as we had hoped, with a devoted dog by their side.

Bobby and Roger moved Ginger to a pen at the racing shop where they worked on cars in the evenings and soldiered on through the following year, helping Ginger stand up, making sure her food and water were close by, and spending more time sitting with her than running as in the past. Finally, the day came when she could no longer get up and stay up, and all of us could see that this was far more humiliating and frustrating for her than it was for us.

When we took her to our new vet, the wife of one of Roger's college friends, we all wrestled with the awareness that we were considering doing for Ginger what we would not have done for a grandparent or any other relative or friend in the same situation. Finally, we agreed, though, that it was time to let Beth put an end to Ginger's pain and frustration.

No matter how we rationalized this, when the day came to say good-bye, it was as difficult as anything we'd ever done, not only because we would miss Ginger terribly, but also because we recognized that she was, in many ways, our last anchor to the childhood of family life that was no more.

Bobby remembers best that last Saturday morning as we sat on the cool cement floor in the basement of Beth's office. Ginger lay across his lap as we petted her and scratched behind her ears. "I remember the look in her eyes," he has said. "She gave me the peace I needed that day, as if to say, 'This is okay. I understand.'"

We buried Ginger in the corner of some land we owned in Chelsea, under a large sweet gum tree, and planted daffodils to brighten the grave when spring came. A very good thing came to our family in a brown paper wrapper at Christmas in 1976. There's no question that she was the best and most meaningful present we ever received—and one that continued to give for many years. As Bobby has put it, "We had a connection, and I still think about her every time I drive through Chelsea."

I do, too.

Another Dog
F. Hopkinson Smith

Do not tell me dogs cannot talk. I know better. I saw it all myself. It was at Sterzing, that most picturesque of all the Tyrolean villages on the Italian slope of the Brenner, with its long, single street, zigzagged like a straggling path in the snow, perhaps it was laid out in that way, and its little open square, with shrine and rude stone fountain, surrounded by women in short skirts and hobnailed shoes, dipping their buckets. On both sides of this street ran queer arcades sheltering shops, their doorways piled with cheap stuffs, fruit, farm implements, and the like, and at the far end, it was almost the last house in the town, stood the old inn, where you breakfast. Such an old, old inn! with swinging sign framed by fantastic iron work, and decorated with overflows of foaming ale in green mugs, crossed clay pipes, and little round dabs of yellow-brown cakes. There was a great archway, too, wide and high, with enormous, barn-like doors fronting on this straggling, zigzag, sabot-trodden street. Under this a cobble-stone pavement led to the door of the coffee-room and out to the stable beyond. These barn-like doors keep out the driving snows and the whirls of sleet and rain, and are slammed to behind horse, sleigh, and all, if not in the face, certainly in the very teeth of the winter gale, while the traveler disentangles his half-frozen legs at his leisure, almost within sight of the blazing fire of the coffee-room within.

Under this great archway, then, against one of these doors, his big paws just inside the shadow line—for it was not winter, but a brilliant summer morning, the grass all dusted with powdered diamonds, the sky a turquoise, the air a joy—under this archway, I say, sat a big St. Bernard dog, squat on his haunches, his head well up, like a grenadier on guard. His eyes commanded the approaches down the road, up the road, and across the street; taking in the passing peddler with the tinware, and the girl with a basket strapped to her back, her fingers knitting for dear life, not to mention so unimportant an object as myself swinging down the road, my iron-shod alpenstock hammering the cobbles.

He made no objection to my entering, neither did he receive me with any show of welcome. There was no bounding forward, no wagging of the tail, no aimless walking around for a moment, and settling down in another spot; nor was there any sudden growl or forbidding look in the eye. None of these things occurred to him, for none of these things was part of his duty. The landlord would do the welcoming, the blue-shirted porter take my knapsack and show me the way to the coffee-room. His business was to sit still and guard that archway. Paying guests, and those known to the family—yes! But stray mountain goats, chickens, inquisitive, pushing peddlers, pigs, and wandering dogs—well, he would look out for these.

While the cutlets and coffee were being fried and boiled, I dragged a chair across the road and tilted it back out of the sun against the wall of a house. I, too, commanded a view down past the blacksmith shop, where they were heating a huge iron tire to clap on the hind wheel of a diligence, and up the street as far as the little square where the women were still clattering about on the cobbles, their buckets on their shoulders. This is how I happened to be watching the dog.

The more I looked at him, the more strongly did his personality impress me. The exceeding gravity of his demeanor! The dignified attitude! The quiet, silent reserve! The way he looked at you from under his eyebrows, not eagerly, nor furtively, but with a self-possessed, competent air, quite like a captain of a Cunarder scanning a horizon from the bridge, or a French gendarme, watching the shifting crowds from one of the little stone circles anchored out in the rush of the boulevards,—a look of authority backed by a sense of unlimited power. Then, too, there was such a dignified cut to his hairy chops as they drooped over his teeth beneath his black, stubby nose. His ears rose and fell easily, without undue haste or excitement when the sound of horses' hoofs put him on his guard, or a goat wandered too near. Yet one could see that he was not a meddlesome dog, nor a snarler, no running out and giving tongue at each passing object, not that kind of a dog at all! He was just a plain, substantial, well-mannered, dignified, self-respecting St. Bernard dog, who knew his place and kept it, who knew his duty and did it, and who would no more chase a cat than he would bite your legs in the dark. Put a cap with a gold band on his head and he would really have made an ideal concierge. Even without the band, he concentrated in his person all the superiority, the repose, and exasperating reticence of that necessary concomitant of Continental hotel life.

Suddenly I noticed a more eager expression on his face. One ear was unfurled, like a flag, and almost run to the masthead; the head was turned quickly down the road. A sound of wheels was heard below the shop. His dogship straightened himself and stood on four legs, his tail wagging slowly.

Another dog was coming.

A great Danish hound, with white eyes, black-and-tan ears, and

23

tail as long and smooth as a policeman's night-club; one of those sleek and shining dogs with powerful chest and knotted legs, a little bowed in front, black lips, and dazzling, fang-like teeth. He was spattered with brown spots, and sported a single white foot. Altogether, he was a dog of quality, of ancestry, of a certain position in his own land—one who had clearly followed his master's mountain wagon to-day as much for love of adventure as anything else. A dog of parts, too, who could perhaps, hunt the wild boar, or give chase to the agile deer. He was certainly not an inn dog. He was rather a palace dog, a chateau, or a shooting-box dog, who, in his off moments, trotted behind hunting carts filled with guns, sportsmen in knee-breeches, or in front of landaus when my lady went an-airing.

And with all this, and quite naturally, he was a dog of breeding, who, while he insisted on his own rights, respected those of others. I saw this before he had spoken ten words to the concierge—the St. Bernard dog, I mean. For he did talk to him, and the conversation was just as plain to me, tilted back against the wall, out of the sun, waiting for my cutlets and coffee, as if I had been a dog myself, and understood each word of it.

First, he walked up sideways, his tail wagging and straight out, like a patent towel-rack. Then he walked round the concierge, who followed his movements with becoming interest, wagging his own tail, straightening his forelegs, and sidling around him kindly, as befitted the stranger's rank and quality, but with a certain dog-independence of manner, preserving his own dignities while courteously passing the time of day, and intimating, by certain twists of his tail, that he felt quite sure his excellency would like the air and scenery the farther he got up the pass—all strange dogs did.

During this interchange of canine civilities, the landlord was helping out the two men, the companions of the dog. One was round and pudgy, the other lank and scrawny. Both were in knickerbockers, with green hats decorated with cock feathers and edelweiss. The blue-shirted porter carried in the bags and alpenstocks, closing the coffee-room door behind them.

Suddenly the strange dog, who had been beguiled by the courteous manner of the concierge, realized that his master had disappeared. The man had been hungry, no doubt, and half blinded by the glare of the sun. After the manner of his kind, he had dived into this shelter without a word to the dumb beast who had tramped behind his wheels, swallowing the dust his horses kicked up.

When the strange dog realized this, I saw the instant the idea entered his mind, as I caught the sudden toss of the head, he glanced quickly about with that uneasy, anxious look that comes into the face of a dog when he discovers that he is adrift in a strange place without his master. What other face is so utterly miserable, and what eyes so pleading, the tears just under the lids, as the lost dog's?

Then it was beautiful to see the St. Bernard. With a sudden twist of the head he reassured the strange dog, telling him, as plainly as could be, not to worry, the gentlemen were only inside, and would be out after breakfast. There was no mistaking what he said. It was done with a peculiar curving of the neck, a reassuring wag of the tail, a glance toward the coffee-room, and a few frolicsome, kittenish jumps, these last plainly indicating that as for himself the occasion was one of great hilarity, with absolutely no cause in it for anxiety. Then, if you could have seen that anxious look fade away from the face of the strange dog, the responsive, reciprocal wag of the night-club of a tail. If you could have caught the sudden peace that came into his eyes, and have seen him as he followed the concierge to the doorway, dropping his ears, and throwing himself beside him, looking up into his face, his tongue out, panting after the habit of his race, the white saliva dropping upon his paws.

Then followed a long talk, conducted in side glances, and punctuated with the quiet laughs of more slappings of tails on the cobbles, as the concierge listened to the adventures of the stranger, or matched them with funny experiences of his own.

Here a whistle from the coffee-room window startled them. Even so rude a being as a man is sometimes mindful of his dog. In an instant both concierge and stranger were on their feet, the concierge ready for whatever would turn up, the stranger trying to locate the sound and his master. Another whistle, and he was off, bounding down the road, looking wistfully at the windows, and rushing back bewildered. Suddenly it came to him that the short cut to his master lay through the archway.

Just here there was a change in the manner of the concierge. It was not gruff, nor savage, nor severe—it was only firm and decided. With his tail still wagging, showing his kindness and willingness to oblige, but with spine rigid and hair bristling, he explained clearly and succinctly to that strange dog how absolutely impossible it would be for him to permit his crossing the archway. Up went the spine of the stranger, and out went his tail like a bar of steel, the feet braced, and the whole body taut as standing rigging. But the concierge kept on wagging his tail, though his hair still bristled, saying as plainly as he could:

"My dear sir, do not blame me. I assure you that nothing in the world would give me more pleasure than to throw the whole house open to you; but consider for a moment. My master puts me here to see that nobody enters the inn but those whom he wishes to see, and that all other live-stock, especially dogs, shall on no account be admitted." (This with head bent on one side and neck arched.) "Now, while I have the most distinguished consideration for your dogship" (tail wagging violently), "and would gladly oblige you, you must see that my honor is at stake" (spine more rigid), "and I feel assured that under the circumstances you will not press a request (low growl) which you must know would be impossible for me to grant."

And the strange dog, gentleman as he was, expressed himself as entirely satisfied with the very free and generous explanation. With tail wagging more violently than ever, he assured the concierge that he understood his position exactly. Then wheeling suddenly, he bounded down the road. Though convinced, he was still anxious.

Then the concierge gravely settled himself once more on his haunches in his customary place, his eyes commanding the view up and down and across the road, where I sat still tilted back in my chair waiting for my cutlets, his whole body at rest, his face expressive of that quiet content which comes from a sense of duties performed and honor untarnished.

But the stranger had duties, too; he must answer the whistle, and find his master. His search down the road being fruitless, he rushed back to the concierge, looking up into his face, his eyes restless and anxious.

"If it were inconsistent with his honor to permit him to cross the threshold, was there any other way he could get into the coffee-room?" This last with a low whine of uneasiness, and a toss of head.

"Yes, certainly," jumping to his feet, "why had he not mentioned it before? It would give him very great pleasure to show him the way to the side entrance." And the St. Bernard, everything wagging now, walked with the stranger to the corner, stopping stock still to point with his nose to the closed door.

Then the stranger bounded down with a scurry and plunge, nervously edging up to the door, wagging his tail, and with a low, anxious whine springing one side and another, his paws now on the sill, his nose at the crack, until the door was finally opened, and he dashed inside.

What happened in the coffee-room I do not know, for I could not see. I am willing, however, to wager that a dog of his loyalty, dignity, and sense of duty did just what a dog of quality would do. No awkward springing at his master's chest with his dusty paws leaving marks on his vest front; no rushing around chairs and tables in mad joy at being let in, alarming waitresses and children. Only a low whine and gurgle of delight, a rubbing of his cold nose against his master's hand, a low, earnest look up into his face, so frank, so trustful, a look that carried no reproach for being shut out, and only gratitude for being let in.

A moment more, and he was outside again, head in air, looking for his friend. Then a dash, and he was around by the archway, licking the concierge in the face, biting his neck, rubbing his nose under his forelegs, saying over and over again how deeply he thanked him,—how glad and proud he was of his acquaintance, and how delighted he would be if he came down to Vienna, or Milan, or wherever he did come from, so that he might return his courtesies in some way, and make his stay pleasant.

Just here the landlord called out that the cutlets and coffee were ready, and, man-like, I went in to breakfast.

Forever Faithful
Karyn Kay Zweifel

"M y God," she said when she had recovered. "Don't sneak up on me like that! How can you move so quietly?"

Claire shrugged, her free arm cradling several stout limbs of respectable size. "I wasn't that quiet," she protested. "Why did you scream?"

"Because you scared me."

"No, not now, before."

Her friend looked at her like she'd lost her mind. "I didn't scream."

"Somebody hollered," Claire said stubbornly. "I heard it. You didn't hear anything?"

Her friend shivered again. "No," she said shortly. "Let's get that fire built, shall we?" With a grand, sweeping gesture, she invited Claire to precede her up the bank to their campsite.

"This isn't enough wood," Claire said.

"There's a tree limb down over there that was too heavy for me. Come on. We can handle it together."

By the time they'd gathered enough wood to suit themselves,

The story of Bill and Callie Sawyers was first told by Margaret Redding Siler in her book *Cherokee Indian Lore and Smoky Mountain Stories* and is retold here with permission.

the forest was enveloped completely in thick, black shadows. Claire giggled as she rummaged through her pack for a flashlight or box of matches.

"It's so dark that I literally can't see my hand in front of my face," she said. "But I can hear that box of matches—it's down near the bottom of my pack."

"Of course," said Natalie. "Anything you really need is at the bottom of the pack—it's Murphy's Law."

They cooked a simple meal of beans and rice, sopping up the juices with thick hunks of French bread. When they finished eating and were sipping coffee to ward off the chill, they built up the fire into a roaring conflagration that seemed to nearly touch the treetops.

"Look at the sparks fly," Claire said dreamily, lying on her back with her bedroll under her head.

Just then a low growl on the trail below made both women sit up. Blood pounded through their veins, and their senses were instantly acute. They listened, but heard nothing more—not even the softest sound of padded footsteps on the forest floor.

"An acoustic trick?" Natalie guessed. "Sound travels better up here?"

Claire shrugged. She sat cross-legged, hunched over her sleeping roll, which was now compressed into a tight little ball in her lap.

"Anything to worry about, Claire?" Natalie's voice quivered a bit.

Claire shrugged again, still listening. Then she forced herself to sound confident. "No big deal, Nat. Maybe some hunter left his dog up here."

Natalie regarded her doubtfully. "They don't allow hunting up here, do they? I'd hate to think we're stuck up here on a mountain miles from anywhere with some whacked-out gun-waving hunter."

"You're right. It was probably some weird acoustic trick, the sound carrying to us from miles away." Claire sat up and dragged the food pack closer to the fire. "Didn't we bring a bottle of brandy?"

They had barely splashed a little brandy into their plastic coffee mugs before there was an explosion of sound on the trail below. They sat, frozen, as a chorus of growls, barks, sharp yips of pain, and occasionally the sickening sound of ripping flesh gave evidence of a mortal battle. The cacophony of pain and anger sounded as if it were no more than ten feet away, just below them on the main path that led down the mountain to their car—and safety.

Finally, the noise died away. Natalie was the first to find her voice. "Claire," she whimpered. She crawled over to her friend, and they just silently held each other, mute with terror.

They shook and rocked, shook and rocked for what seemed to be an eternity. The fire threw out a meager circle of light, illuminating their tent and an area a few feet beyond. Past the firelight was a darkness so black that not even the shadows moved. It was more than an absence of light—the darkness was a palpable, living entity, with a texture like fur and a smell like fear. The two women were utterly, totally isolated.

"Howdy." The figure broke loose from the blackness, pulling free from the shadows and slowly, hesitantly edging toward the warmth and light of the fire.

The sudden deadweight of Claire in her arms somehow translated into a coherent thought in Natalie's mind: "She's fainted—now we're both going to die." She clenched her eyes shut as tightly as she could and thought again, "Dear God, why can't I think of anything to say to You?" The words "we who are about to die salute you" ran through her mind, but she dismissed them impatiently—that was something Roman gladiators said to the emperor. "Is there nothing to say? Am I going to die with all these stupid thoughts running through my head?" she thought.

Nothing happened. No earth-shattering revelations, but no bright, blinding flash of pain either. Natalie slit open one eye to see if she had only hallucinated the presence of a strange old man thirty miles from the nearest town and ten miles up from any passable road.

He was hunkered down by the fire, examining the lightweight plastic bottle they'd carried the brandy in. As she watched, he snapped off the top and sniffed.

"Mind if I try some?" He gestured with the bottle in Natalie's direction, and she squeezed her eyes shut again. Her mind's eye flashed on a possum she'd seen once, its stiff, anxious posture such a ridiculous commentary on its hopeless, uncontrollable desire to live that she had snorted in laughter. She saw herself as that possum now, and although she could not laugh, she could at least force her eyes to open and face whatever lay ahead.

"Sure," she croaked. Claire stirred beneath her and then raised her head, cracking it resoundingly on Natalie's elbow. They both howled in pain, tears coming up quick and hot, while the man surveyed them over the neck of the bottle.

"That smarts," he commented when the two women had calmed down enough to hear him.

"Who are you?" Claire's tone was menacing enough, but her body posture gave her away. She was trying to unobtrusively scoot backward on her rear end.

"Ed." He grinned, and they could see neat little squares of lightlessness, just like the night beyond the campfire, irregularly spaced within his mouth. "Ed Welch. This stuff tastes like lighter fluid." He gestured with the bottle, and the women saw that two-thirds of its contents were gone.

Natalie was beyond being afraid. "Where did you come from?" she demanded.

"Over next ridge a ways. Didn't mean to scare you."

His gaze fell over Natalie to the tent behind her. She turned to see Claire, still sitting and scooting, duck out from the flaps with the flashlight in her hand.

"You'd just better sit still, mister." Claire's tone was still threatening, and now she had a weapon of sorts to back it up.

He threw up his hands, and Natalie noticed suddenly how thin he was. "I don't mean you any harm, really I don't."

"But where did you come from?" Natalie repeated stupidly.

"Over yonder." He pointed again, patiently.

"Why did you come this way? Where are you going?"

"Ssshh." The man was instantly alert, cocking his head to listen. From the trail below came a short series of yips, whines, and yelps. Two dogs, by the sound of it, confused or hurt or both.

The women tensed, and Claire let the flashlight hang down by her side, forgotten and useless against this unseen threat.

The noise died away. The man relaxed, his long bony hands dangling over his knees.

"What was that?" Natalie whispered.

"Them's Bill Sawyers' dogs," he replied matter-of-factly. "They'll be at it all night, most likely."

"What's wrong with them?" Claire was intrigued in spite of herself. The man shrugged. "Can't rest, I reckon."

"What do you mean?"

"It was a terrible thing." He shook his head and then raised the bottle again. "Can I?"

The two women nodded, nearly spellbound by this apparition in the wilderness.

"Bill got up about sunrise one morning and decided to go check on some calves up in the pastures. You know he kept cattle for Jess Siler?"

The women nodded again, since this seemed to be the anticipated response. Natalie wondered for the first time if this man was all right in the head.

"There was bear up here then and wolves and wildcats that'd take a calf or about anything they thought they could get away with. So Bill kissed Callie goodbye, whistled up his dogs, and told the children to mind their ma. Let's see, there was..." He whispered to himself and counted on his fingers before continuing. "There were nine of them—nine children in all.

"Bill had lots of dogs, too, for hunting, herding cattle, guarding the cabin, you know. But his two favorite dogs were Lead and Larry. Lead was a big blue-spotted hound, sort of, but really mostly mutt. Larry was just an old black-and-tan dog, floppy ears, and long legs. They loved that man, and he all but let them sleep in the bed with him and Callie—Callie drew the line at that. She was a Welch, come right down to it, and that meant she could be pretty doggone stubborn."

Again the man grinned. Natalie's eyes were drawn to the intricate network of wrinkles that crisscrossed his face, radiating from the edges of his mouth and the corners of his eyes.

"Bill told her he'd be back by dinnertime, or maybe supper if the calves had strayed any. Callie watched him walk out onto that trail that twisted and turned up to the high meadows where sweet grass grows, and then she turned to her own work. There was nothing at all unusual about his leaving.

"When supper came and there was no Bill to say the blessing,

Callie was a bit uneasy. The children were quick to pick up her share, so she put it behind her for their sakes. She probably told them stories before they went to sleep—she was good at telling stories.

"Sometimes storytelling reaches back and bites you, though, because she told me that she couldn't sleep a wink that night. She kept thinking up reasons why Bill hadn't come home, and every story made her more worried. She would jump at the least little sound thinking it was him on the path, but it never was. Poor Callie—it was the longest night.

"When the sun first started coming up, Callie jumped right out of bed and stirred up the fire—October mornings get pretty chilly. While she was putting breakfast on, she heard a scratching at the door. So worried about Bill that she could hardly think straight, Callie ran right over and opened it up. On the doorstep was old Lead, the blue-spotted dog. She was glad to see him and called out his name, thinking Bill would be right along in a minute.

"But Lead was acting real funny. He whined and ran up the path a ways and came back whining. When he ran up the path and barked, it was clear as day that he wanted her to follow him. Well, Callie grabbed her wrap and a piece of pone bread and ran out the door—she was so eager to go find Bill. She tossed Lead the bread as a reward, but he didn't gobble it down. He carried it real careful in his mouth and trotted up the path and around a bend.

"Callie followed along behind Lead, and the farther they went, the heavier her heart got. She just started knowing, somehow, that things were not right. The trail twisted and turned, and once, near the top of the ridge, she lost sight of Lead. Then she heard the boisterous barking of Larry, and she started running to the turn in the trail.

"Bill was there. His body was cold, and his face was all screwed up like he'd had an awful lot of pain. But his footsteps and the dogs' paw prints were the only marks on the trail, and there wasn't a mark on Bill, so Callie figured he'd died of the cramps. They call it appenda-something now, I think. Hurts like the devil but can't kill you if you see a doctor quick."

The old man's audience sat, truly spellbound now, having edged their way to the fire's side. They could only nod and murmur, caught up in his story.

"Out of the corner of her eye, Callie saw Lead drop something and Larry turn it over with his nose. It was the hunk of bread she'd given Lead back at the cabin, and she watched, amazed, as Larry carefully bit the piece of food in half, leaving Lead a share.

"I imagine she cried a little to see these two good dogs that had stayed by their master all through the night. And you know how animals are—they understand how you feel. Larry came over to her as she sat with Bill's head in her lap and lay down, pressing close against her while she cried. Lead stood over her shoulder and leaned on her while he cried a little, too. They were mostly confused, though, like they just didn't know why Bill didn't get up and go on.

"Pretty soon Callie dried her tears and started thinking what could she do. Bill was a big man, and she couldn't carry him down the mountain—she had to get some help from another adult. Her sons, her oldest ones that is, were just thirteen and eleven. Her brother Bert lived twelve miles away, and he could help her do what needed to be done to get Bill taken care of.

"Looking up at the sun, she decided she had just enough time before dark to get her children to Bert's cabin. She kissed Bill and laid his hat across his face, but she hated to leave him there alone. She told those dogs very firmly to stay, and although she could tell they wanted to come with her, they did, finally, sit down next to Bill's body. That was a sight she would remember the rest of her life: her tall, lanky husband lying in the middle of the path, flanked by those two loyal creatures sitting proud and tall."

A growl came from the trail below, sounding as close as the edge of the circle of light thrown by the fire. Natalie jumped and shrieked softly, her fingers digging into the soft flesh of Claire's arm. Claire, too, paled, and the storyteller smiled, exposing again those coal black gaping holes between his teeth.

"Callie was a strong woman, and she did not panic or make the children afraid. She took the older ones aside and told them that their pa had died and they had to get to Uncle Bert's before dark. The older ones helped the younger ones, and Callie wrapped up the baby in her shawl. They left the cabin pretty quick and struck out through the mountains. They had to walk fast to get there safely before dark, and it's a long, hard hike even for folks with long legs. Sometimes the little ones would cry, and the bigger ones would have to try to carry them. Callie, of course, was carrying the baby and the rifle and sometimes even one of the little toddlers. With nine children and only two of them over ten, it was not an easy trip.

"At last they were on the ridge across from the cabin. The sun had just gone beyond the mountain, and the shadows were growing fast. Callie hollered and the boys hollered, and pretty soon, Bert hollered back. Him and his wife came to help her get the kids inside, and the children were able to rest. Their aunt fed them a warm meal while Callie told Bert what had happened.

"Bert left at first light the next morning to go to his neighbor's house and get a couple more men. Then they'd all go to get Bill and carry him down to his cabin. Bert's son tagged along, working hard to keep up, trying to match his pa's long stride up and down the mountainside.

"They stopped at Bill and Callie's cabin, like Callie had told them to, so they could get a quilt to wrap Bill in and some bread to feed Larry and Lead—Callie knew those dogs wouldn't have left Bill to look for food.

"We found Bill pretty much as Callie'd described him—lying in the middle of the trail with his hat over his face, a few leaves blown over him. But the trail around him was all churned up, with paw prints crossing and crisscrossing in the dirt. A panther, its throat savagely ripped open, lay underneath the big hemlock tree not five feet from Bill's body. And Larry and Lead, still sitting on either side of their master, were horribly torn up. Long, raking claw marks still dripped blood from their sides, Larry had an ear that was nearly torn off, and Lead had an eye that was nearly swollen shut.

"We threw the bread to them, and they limped up to get it, sharing it just like when Callie had given them a piece, and then they turned and went back to their posts by Bill's side. We went a little farther up the trail and found the bodies of two wildcats, both bearing the unmistakable marks of good old Larry and Lead.

"Of course the wildcats and the panther had smelled Bill's body, and it smelled like supper to them. But Larry and Lead fought like wild things themselves and saved Bill from getting all torn up.

"We started to go up to Bill's body to wrap him in the quilt and carry him home, but Larry and Lead sprang at us as quick as you please. They were going to rip our throats out, too, most likely— they'd fought like crazy all night long to protect their master, and we were just another threat in their eyes. They didn't know we didn't mean him any harm.

"We tried sweet-talking them and ordering them and tricking them away from the body, but they weren't going to budge. Finally, Bert said we'd just have to shoot them so we could get the body home. It was getting dark, and there were plenty of other wildcats around.

"Nobody wanted to shoot Larry and Lead. Not even Bert could bring himself to do it because he knew those poor dogs were only doing what they thought was right. We were all relieved to hear another dog barking down the trail. Larry and Lead seemed to recognize the bark, and they stood up and began to wag their tails and sort of yip in return. I ran down the trail and found a man who'd helped Bill with the cattle before. His dog knew Larry and Lead, and he knew Bill's dogs too.

"Cade, that's his name, he gentled those dogs, talking to them real soft and telling them how sorry he was about Bill. He went up and stroked Bill's face and cried a little, and the dogs moaned, too. Soon enough, he'd convinced those dogs that he meant Bill no harm, and they let him gather Bill up in his arms and walk on down the trail. Those dogs walked right alongside him, proud and sad all at the same time.

"They had a right to lead that funeral procession if anybody did. Bloody, battered, and weak from hunger and lack of water, they finally saw to it that Bill got home."

A low growl erupted from the shadows. Then a bloodcurdling shriek filled the air, followed by more howls, low, murderous growls, and the sharp, ripping sounds of teeth making contact with flesh. The old man sat by the fire, a faraway smile on his face. Claire crept off to the tent and grabbed the two sleeping bags; the women wrapped themselves against the evening chill, and the three kept vigil until the sun came up, listening to the intermittent, savage battle being relived on the trail below.

The old man disappeared shortly after sunrise, and the women broke down their camp and continued on their way. Claire was inclined to believe that the old man was a figment of their imagination, but Natalie argued fiercely that he was real.

"Nobody but a real, live human being could have b.o. like that," she said firmly. "And I don't think a ghost drank all our brandy, either."

They were subdued for the next two days. When they hiked out of the woods and back to their car, they had only three things on their minds: a hot meal, a hot bath, and a warm, soft bed. They drove to the little diner in the nearest town.

"You girls been on the trail long?" asked the waitress, filling their coffee cups for the fourth time and surveying their disheveled appearance with some amusement.

"Three days," Claire confirmed, between heaping forkfuls of boiled cabbage and corned beef.

Natalie had taken the edge off her hunger already. "You go up there much?" she asked the waitress as she waved her fork vaguely toward the mountains and the trail they'd followed.

The woman laughed. "God love you, I was raised up there, and I like it right where I am now, thank you."

"Anybody still live up there?" continued Natalie. Claire saw the gleam in her eye that meant she was engaged in more than idle conversation.

The woman shook her head, backing away from the table. "That's a national park or some such, now. You know that."

"But does anybody live up there?"

The woman started to turn and leave, muttering something about customers, although Natalie and Claire were the only people in the little cafe. "Wait," Natalie urged. "I'm not trying to be nosy or get anybody in trouble. It's just that something really weird happened to us up there." The woman turned back and pinned Natalie with a look that was almost unfriendly.

"An old man came up to us and started telling us stories," Claire interrupted. "But he couldn't have been real, could he?"

The woman's face softened. "Old Ed Welch is real, all right," she said. "Real ornery, but they say that's what it takes to live as long as he has."

"How old is he?" Natalie couldn't resist a triumphant poke to Claire's ribs.

"Probably just a hair shy of a hundred or maybe more than a hundred." The waitress shrugged. "Nobody really knows. But he's crazy as a loon. I wouldn't believe a word he told you if I were you."

Claire poked Natalie, triumphant in her turn. "He told us some stupid story about a man and his dogs."

The waitress sat the coffeepot down on the table behind them and reached into her apron for their check.

"Well, now, I reckon that's the only true story Ed Welch knows," she admitted. "Bill Sawyers and his family were good people."

"It really happened?"

"Yes, ma'am, it did." The waitress placed the check on the table with a note of finality. "Hope you enjoyed your dinner. Come back again, anytime."

On a Dog and a Man Also
Hilaire Belloc

There lives in the middle of the Weald upon the northern edge of a small wood where a steep brow of orchard pasture goes down to a little river, a Recluse who is of middle age and possessed of all the ordinary accomplishments; that is, French and English literature are familiar to him, he can himself compose, he has read his classical Latin and can easily decipher such Greek as he has been taught in youth. He is unmarried, he is by birth a gentleman, he enjoys an income sufficient to give him food and wine, and has for companion a dog who, by the standard of dogs, is somewhat more elderly than himself.

This dog is called Argus, not that he has a hundred eyes nor even two, indeed he has but one; for the other, or right eye, he lost the sight of long ago from luxury and lack of exercise. This dog Argus is neither small nor large; he is brown in colour and covered—though now but partially—with curly hair. In this he resembles many other dogs, but he differs from most of his breed in a further character, which is that by long association with a Recluse he has acquired a human manner that is unholy. He is fond of affected poses. When he sleeps it is with that abandonment of fatigue only naturally to be found in mankind. He watches sunsets and listens mournfully to music. Cooked food is dearer to him than raw, and he will eat nuts—a monstrous thing in a dog and proof of corruption.

Nevertheless, or, rather, on account of all this, the dog Argus is exceedingly dear to his master, and of both I had the other day a singular revelation when I set out at evening to call upon my friend.

The sun had set, but the air was still clear and it was light enough to have shot a bat (had there been bats about and had one had a gun) when I knocked at the cottage door and opened it. Right within, one comes to the first of the three rooms which the Recluse possesses, and there I found him tenderly nursing the dog Argus, who lay groaning in the arm-chair and putting on all the airs of a Christian man at the point of death.

The Recluse did not even greet me, but asked me only in a hurried way how I thought the dog Argus looked. I answered gravely and in a low tone so as not to disturb the sufferer, that as I had not seen him since Tuesday, when he was, for an elderly dog, in the best of health, he certainly presented a sad contrast, but that perhaps he was better than he had been some few hours before, and that the Recluse himself would be the best judge of that.

My friend was greatly relieved at what I said, and told me that he thought the dog was better, compared at least with that same morning; then, whether you believe it or not, he took him by the left leg just above the paw and held it for a little time as though he were feeling a pulse, and said, "He came back less than twenty-four hours ago!" It seemed that the dog Argus, for the first time in fourteen years, had run away, and that for the first time in perhaps twenty or thirty years the emotion of loss had entered into the life of the Recluse, and that he had felt something outside books and outside the contemplation of the landscape about his hermitage.

In a short time the dog fell into a slumber, as was shown by a number of grunts and yaps which proved his sleep, for the dog

On a Dog and a Man Also

Argus is of that kind which hunts in dreams. His master covered him reverently rather than gently with an Indian cloth and, still leaving him in the armchair, sat down upon a common wooden chair close by and gazed pitifully at the fire. For my part I stood up and wondered at them both, and wondered also at that in man by which he must attach himself to something, even if it be but a dog, a politician, or an ungrateful child.

When he had gazed at the fire a little while the Recluse began to talk, and I listened to him talking:

"Even if they had not dug up so much earth to prove it I should have known," said he, "that the Odyssey was written not at the beginning of a civilisation nor in the splendour of it, but towards its close. I do not say this from the evening light that shines across its pages, for that is common to all profound work, but I say it because of the animals, and especially because of the dog, who was the only one to know his master when that master came home a beggar to his own land, before his youth was restored to him, and before he got back his women and his kingship by the bending of his bow, and before he hanged the housemaids and killed all those who had despised him."

"But how," said I (for I am younger than he), "can the animals in the poem show you that the poem belongs to a decline?"

"Why," said he, "because at the end of a great civilisation the air gets empty, the light goes out of the sky, the gods depart, and men in their loneliness put out a groping hand, catching at the friendship of, and trying to understand, whatever lives and suffers as they do. You will find it never fail that where a passionate regard for the animals about us, or even a great tenderness for them, is to be found there is also to be found decay in the State."

"I hope not," said I. "Moreover, it cannot be true, for in the Thirteenth Century, which was certainly the healthiest time we ever

45

had, animals were understood; and I will prove it to you in several carvings."

He shrugged his shoulders and shook his head, saying, "In the rough and in general it is true; and the reason is the reason I have given you, that when decay begins, whether of a man or of a State, there comes with it an appalling and a torturing loneliness in which our energies decline into a strong affection for whatever is constantly our companion and for whatever is certainly present upon earth. For we have lost the sky."

"Then if the senses are so powerful in a decline of the State there should come at the same time," said I, "a quick forgetfulness of the human dead and an easy change of human friendship?"

"There does," he answered, and to that there was no more to be said.

"I know it by my own experience," he continued. "When, yesterday, at sunset, I looked for my dog Argus and could not find him, I went out into the wood and called him: the darkness came and I found no trace of him. I did not hear him barking far off as I have heard him before when he was younger and went hunting for a while, and three times that night I came back out of the wild into the warmth of my house, making sure he would have returned, but he was never there. The third time I had gone a mile out to the gamekeeper's to give him money if Argus should be found, and I asked him as many questions and as foolish as a woman would ask. Then I sat up right into the night, thinking that every movement of the wind outside or of the drip of water was the little pad of his step coming up the flagstones to the door. I was even in the mood when men see unreal things, and twice I thought I saw him passing quickly between my chair and the passage to the further room. But these things are proper to the night and the strongest thing I suffered for him was in the morning.

"It was, as you know, very bitterly cold for several days. They found things dead in the hedgerows, and there was perhaps no running water between here and the Downs. There was no shelter from the snow. There was no cover for my friend at all. And when I was up at dawn with the faint light about, a driving wind full of sleet filled all the air. Then I made certain that the dog Argus was dead, and what was worse that I should not find his body: that the old dog had got caught in some snare or that his strength had failed him through the cold, as it fails us human beings also upon such nights, striking at the heart.

"Though I was certain that I would not see him again yet I went on foolishly and aimlessly enough, plunging through the snow from one spinney to another and hoping that I might hear a whine. I heard none: and if the little trail he had made in his departure might have been seen in the evening, long before that morning the drift would have covered it.

"I had eaten nothing and yet it was near noon when I returned, pushing forward to the cottage against the pressure of the storm, when I found there, miserably crouched, trembling, half dead, in the lee of a little thick yew beside my door, the dog Argus; and as I came his tail just wagged and he just moved his ears, but he had not the strength to come near me, his master."

"I carried him in and put him here, feeding him by force, and I have restored him."

All this the Recluse said to me with as deep and as restrained emotion as though he had been speaking of the most sacred things, as indeed, for him, these things were sacred.

It was therefore a mere inadvertence in me, and an untrained habit of thinking aloud, which made me say:

"Good Heavens, what will you do when the dog Argus dies?"

At once I wished I had not said it, for I could see that the

Recluse could not bear the words. I looked therefore a little awkwardly beyond him and was pleased to see the dog Argus lazily opening his one eye and surveying me with torpor and with contempt. He was certainly less moved than his master.

Then in my heart I prayed that of these two (unless The God would make them both immortal and catch them up into whatever place is better than the Weald, or unless he would grant them one death together upon one day) that the dog Argus might survive my friend, and that the Recluse might be the first to dissolve that long companionship. For of this I am certain, that the dog would suffer less; for men love their dependents much more than do their dependents them; and this is especially true of brutes; for men are nearer to the gods.

A Back Porch Dog
Becky Hutto

I don't remember when I first saw him, but I do remember one of the first times I actually got to know him. My brother had purchased a new home, complete with a fenced backyard and he wasted no time in buying a puppy. I arrived at my brother's house and no one was home but Bailey. He was in the backyard and was very happy to see me, even though I was someone he did not know very well. I remember how he put his paws up on the fence and wanted immediate "loving." But what I remember most about getting to know Bailey was his happy face. He had a continual smile.

Soon after my mother died, my brother asked what I thought about having Bailey move in with our dad. Daddy loved Bailey— that was quite obvious. He seemed to enjoy being with him the times Bailey had visited. I thought it was a great idea. My brother had acquired two additional dogs and felt that Bailey would not get the one-on-one attention he needed. He knew that Bailey would demand it, and my dad would give him, more than enough attention and love.

Bailey moved to Parrish and within no time he and my dad were friends. Every Friday that I talked with my dad, he had another Bailey story to tell me. The two of them lived happily on

Bank Street. Everyone who drove into the backyard was greeted by a happy golden retriever.

There are so many Bailey stories to remember. Phyllis, the lady who cooked for Dad, always cooked extra for Bailey. On the days she cooked, Bailey's meals included butter beans, meatloaf—everything that Dad ate. He especially enjoyed her desserts. He also got a regular breakfast from the neighbor across the street. Bailey would look at the kitchen window to see if my dad was watching, then slip across the street to get his free breakfast and come right back to his porch.

My dad always complained that he could not work in his woodshop because Bailey was right under foot. That was true. Every minute that he was outside, Bailey was right by his side. Once my dad fell while outside and he was unable to get up because Bailey was licking him so hard on the face.

One big project that Dad had worked on was to relocate Bailey's doghouse. It seemed that somehow Bailey had located the window to my dad's bedroom and decided to sleep there next to the house. He even worked to dig a little hole right under the window. My dad understood what Bailey had done, so he simply moved his doghouse to the exact location so Bailey could sleep inside the doghouse, and still be under the bedroom window.

My dad went to the hospital in November for the last time. He was working on a new, very nice and roomy doghouse for Bailey the day he got sick. Of course, Bailey and the family did not know that it was the end; he had been to the hospital several times since Bailey had been there. Each time Dad had been away, Bailey stayed on the back porch, waiting on his return. Many friends and family members took care of him and neighbors kept watch on him. He always waited patiently for Daddy to return.

I stayed with Bailey for a few nights during my dad's last illness.

A Back Porch Dog

One morning I was waiting for my cousin to take me to the hospital and I got up early. I fed Bailey and he and I decided to play ball in the backyard, one of his favorite things to do early in the morning! I would throw the ball and he would bring it back to me, drop it at my feet, and look inside the kitchen door. He was trying to see if someone else was in the house. He was looking for Dad, his best friend. It broke my heart and I did not stay there alone again.

My dad was in the hospital on Thanksgiving Day, and a friend went by his house to spend time with Bailey. She and her niece played ball with him and took a good picture of a happy Bailey, playing hard in his backyard. She made a copy of that picture and took it to the hospital. I was in Dad's room when he saw the picture for the first time. His face lit up in a special way, he was so glad to see a picture of Bailey. He was moved back and forth from a regular room to intensive care several times and with each move, the picture of Bailey went with him. All the nurses and doctors commented on what a good picture and Dad was proud to tell them that was his dog—Bailey. He never went into a lot of details with dog stories, but looking at his face when he saw that picture told the story.

The day after Daddy died, I went back to the house and there was Bailey, still on the porch. When I drove up, the neighbor across the street came over to talk. This neighbor had known my family for a long time and like most small town residents, she knew a lot about what went on. She told me that she had been at church choir practice on the Wednesday night that Daddy died. The choir members knew that he was close to death and they found out he had died before they left church.

When she got home, she saw that no one was at our house, but later, around 10:00 p.m., a car pulled up in Dad's backyard. The neighbor, Mrs. Dunn, looked out her window to see if it might be me or my brother. She was confused since she did not recognize the car or the person who got out of the car. Living in a small town, that was quite remarkable, that someone would come to Dad's house and she not know who they were.

A woman got out of the car and Mrs. Dunn noticed that she had a bowl in her hand. Mrs. Dunn, not afraid to be the helpful (nosey) neighbor, went out on her porch and asked the visitor if she could help her. The person said she had just heard that Mr. Martin died. Mrs. Dunn told her that was correct. The woman said, "I wanted to do something and all I could think about was fixing some food for Bailey. Do you think that is okay?" Mrs. Dunn, told her, of course, that was fine, then went back inside and watched through her window. The weather for that particular December night had been bad—there had been a cold rain off and on all day and night. The girl that she did not know and that she had never seen before, sat on the back porch, in the cold, dark December night while Bailey ate a special supper. After she petted him for a while, she got back in her car and left.

I wonder if Bailey knew why he had an unexpected guest late that night. I wonder if he knew that Daddy had died. I don't know. That was on a Wednesday and on that following Sunday, Bailey moved in to live with me. My husband's brother went by and picked him up, complete with his dog food bowl, leash, and everything that was his, and brought him to my house. I was still numb from everything that had happened, but I felt so relieved to have him because I knew I could give him my heart. Bailey and I needed each other.

Bailey acted sad the first few weeks, even months, until we had a good schedule, and until he felt secure, but now he seems to be happy. I do look at him a lot, when he is lying on the floor. He will cross his paws, put his head on them, and look like he is thinking, like he is remembering. I wonder if he thinks about Parrish and the back porch. I know I do, but now we have each other. Daddy would be glad to know Bailey has a home.

Our Friend the Dog
Maurice Maeterlinck

I

I have lost, within these last few days, a little bull-dog. He had just completed the sixth month of his brief existence. He had no history. His intelligent eyes opened to look out upon the world, to love mankind, then closed again on the cruel secrets of death.

The friend who presented me with him had given him, perhaps by antiphrasis, the startling name of Pelléas. Why rechristen him? For how can a poor dog, loving, devoted, faithful, disgrace the name of a man or an imaginary hero?

Pelléas had a great bulging, powerful forehead, like that of Socrates or Verlaine; and, under a little black nose, blunt as a churlish assent, a pair of large hanging and symmetrical chops, which made his head a sort of massive, obstinate, pensive and three-cornered menace. He was beautiful after the manner of a beautiful, natural monster that has complied strictly with the laws of its species. And what a smile of attentive obligingness, of incorruptible innocence, of affectionate submission, of boundless gratitude and total self-abandonment lit up, at the least caress, that adorable mask of ugliness! Whence exactly did that smile emanate? From the ingenuous and melting eyes? From the ears pricked up to catch the words of man? From the forehead that unwrinkled to appreciate and love, or from the stump of a tail that wriggled at the other end to testify to the intimate and impassioned joy that filled his small being, happy once more to encounter the hand or the glance of the god to whom he surrendered himself?

Pelléas was born in Paris, and I had taken him to the country. His bonny fat paws, shapeless and not yet stiffened, carried slackly through the unexplored pathways of his new existence his huge and serious head, flat-nosed and, as it were, rendered heavy with thought.

For this thankless and rather sad head, like that of an overworked child, was beginning the overwhelming work that oppresses every brain at the start of life. He had, in less than five or six weeks, to get into his mind, taking shape within it, an image and a satisfactory conception of the universe. Man, aided by all the knowledge of his own elders and his brothers, takes thirty or forty years to outline that conception, but the humble dog has to unravel it for himself in a few days: and yet, in the eyes of a god, who should know all things, would it not have the same weight and the same value as our own?

It was a question, then, of studying the ground, which can be scratched and dug up and which sometimes reveals surprising things; of casting at the sky, which is uninteresting, for there is nothing there to eat, one glance that does away with it for good and all; of discovering the grass, the admirable and green grass, the springy and cool grass, a field for races and sports, a friendly and boundless bed, in which lies hidden the good and wholesome couch-grass. It was a question, also, of taking promiscuously a thousand urgent and curious observations. It was necessary, for instance, with no other guide than pain, to learn to calculate the height of objects from the top of which you can jump into space; to convince yourself that it is vain to pursue birds who fly away and that you are unable to clamber up trees after the cats who defy you there; to distinguish between the sunny spots where it is delicious to sleep and the patches of shade in which you shiver; to remark with stupefaction that the rain does not fall inside the houses, that water is cold, uninhabitable and dangerous, while fire is beneficent at a distance, but terrible when you come too near; to observe that the meadows, the farm-yards and sometimes the roads are haunted by giant creatures with threatening horns, creatures good-natured, perhaps, and, at any rate, silent, creatures who allow you to sniff at them a little curiously without taking offence, but who keep their real thoughts to themselves. It was necessary to learn, as the result of painful and humiliating experiment, that you are not at liberty to obey all nature's laws without distinction in the dwelling of the gods; to recognize that the kitchen is the privileged and most agreeable spot in that divine dwelling, although you are hardly allowed to abide in it because of the cook, who is a considerable, but jealous power; to learn that doors are important and capricious volitions, which sometimes lead to felicity, but which most often, hermetically closed, mute and stern, haughty and heartless, remain deaf to all entreaties; to admit, once and for all, that the essential good things of life, the indisputable blessings, generally imprisoned in pots and stewpans, are almost always inaccessible; to know how to look at them with laboriously-acquired indifference and to practise to take no notice of them, saying to yourself that here are objects which are probably sacred, since merely to skim them with the tip of a respectful tongue is enough to let loose the unanimous anger of all the gods of the house.

And then, what is one to think of the table on which so many things happen that cannot be guessed; of the derisive chairs on which one is forbidden to sleep; of the plates and dishes that are empty by the time that one can get at them; of the lamp that drives away the dark?...How many orders, dangers, prohibitions, problems, enigmas has one not to classify in one's overburdened memory!...And how to reconcile all this with other laws, other enigmas, wider and more imperious, which one bears within one's self, within one's instinct, which spring up and develop from one hour to the other, which come from the depths of time and the race, invade the blood, the muscles and the nerves and suddenly assert themselves more irresistibly and more powerfully than pain, the word of the master himself, or the fear of death?

Thus, for instance, to quote only one example, when the hour of sleep has struck for men, you have retired to your hole, surrounded by the darkness, the silence and the formidable solitude of the night. All is sleep in the master's house. You feel yourself very small and weak in the presence of the mystery. You know that the gloom is peopled with foes who hover and lie in wait. You suspect the trees, the passing wind and the moonbeams. You would like to hide, to suppress yourself by holding your breath. But still the watch must be kept; you must, at the least sound, issue from your retreat, face the invisible and bluntly disturb the imposing silence of the earth, at the risk of bringing down the whispering evil or crime upon yourself alone. Whoever the enemy be, even if he be man, that is to say, the very brother of the god whom it is your business to defend, you must attack him blindly, fly at his throat, fasten your perhaps sacrilegious teeth into human flesh, disregard the spell of a hand and voice similar to those of your master, never be silent, never attempt to escape, never allow yourself to be tempted or bribed and, lost in the night without help, prolong the heroic alarm to your last breath.

There is the great ancestral duty, the essential duty, stronger than death, which not even man's will and anger are able to check.

Our Friend the Dog

All our humble history, linked with that of the dog in our first struggles against every breathing thing, tends to prevent his forgetting it. And when, in our safer dwelling-places of to-day, we happen to punish him for his untimely zeal, he throws us a glance of astonished reproach, as though to point out to us that we are in the wrong and that, if we lose sight of the main clause in the treaty of alliance which he made with us at the time when we lived in caves, forests and fens, he continues faithful to it in spite of us and remains nearer to the eternal truth of life, which is full of snares and hostile forces.

But how much care and study are needed to succeed in fulfilling this duty! And how complicated it has become since the days of the silent caverns and the great deserted lakes! It was all so simple, then, so easy and so clear. The lonely hollow opened upon the side of the hill, and all that approached, all that moved on the horizon of the plains or woods, was the unmistakable enemy....But to-day you can no longer tell....You have to acquaint yourself with a civilization of which you disapprove, to appear to understand a thousand incomprehensible things....Thus, it seems evident that henceforth the whole world no longer belongs to the master, that his property conforms to unintelligible limits.... It becomes necessary, therefore, first of all to know exactly where the sacred domain begins and ends. Whom are you to suffer, whom to stop?...There is the road by which every one, even the poor, has the right to pass. Why? You do not know; it is a fact which you deplore, but which you are bound to accept. Fortunately, on the other hand, here is the fair path which none may tread. This path is faithful to the sound traditions; it is not to be lost sight of; for by it enter into your daily existence the difficult problems of life.

Would you have an example? You are sleeping peacefully in a ray of the sun that covers the threshold of the kitchen with pearls.

The earthenware pots are amusing themselves by elbowing and nudging one another on the edge of the shelves trimmed with paper lace-work. The copper stewpans play at scattering spots of light over the smooth white walls. The motherly stove hums a soft tune and dandles three saucepans blissfully dancing; and, from the little hole that lights up its inside, defies the good dog who cannot approach, by constantly putting out at him its fiery tongue. The clock, bored in its oak case, before striking the august hour of meal time, swings its great gilt navel to and fro; and the cunning flies tease your ears. On the glittering table lie a chicken, a hare, three partridges, besides other things which are called fruits—peaches, melons, grapes—and which are all good for nothing. The cook guts a big silver fish and throws the entrails (instead of giving them to you!) into the dust-bin. Ah, the dust-bin! Inexhaustible treasury, receptacle of windfalls, the jewel of the house! You shall have your share of it, an exquisite and surreptitious share; but it does not do to seem to know where it is. You are strictly forbidden to rummage in it. Man in this way prohibits many pleasant things, and life would be dull indeed and your days empty if you had to obey all the orders of the pantry, the cellar and the dining-room. Luckily, he is absent-minded and does not long remember the instructions which he lavishes. He is easily deceived. You achieve your ends and do as you please, provided you have the patience to await the hour. You are subject to man, and he is the one god; but you none the less have your own personal, exact and imperturbable morality, which proclaims aloud that illicit acts become most lawful through the very fact that they are performed without the master's knowledge. Therefore, let us close the watchful eye that has seen. Let us pretend to sleep and to dream of the moon....

Hark! A gentle tapping at the blue window that looks out on the garden! What is it? Nothing; a bough of hawthorn that has come to see what we are doing in the cool kitchen. Trees are inquisitive and often excited; but they do not count, one has nothing to say to them, they are irresponsible, they obey the wind, which has no principles....But what is that? I hear steps!...Up, ears open; nose on the alert!... It is the baker coming up to the rails, while the postman is opening a little gate in the hedge of lime-trees. They are friends; it is well; they bring something: you can greet them and wag your tail discreetly twice or thrice, with a patronizing smile....

Another alarm! What is it now? A carriage pulls up in front of the steps. The problem is a complex one. Before all, it is of consequence to heap copious insults on the horses, great, proud beasts, who make no reply. Meantime, you examine out of the corner of your eye the persons alighting. They are well-clad and seem full of confidence. They are probably going to sit at the table of the gods. The proper thing is to bark without acrimony, with a shade of respect, so as to show that you are doing your duty, but that you are doing it with intelligence. Nevertheless, you cherish a lurking suspicion and, behind the guests' backs, stealthily, you sniff the air persistently and in a knowing way, in order to discern any hidden intentions.

But halting footsteps resound outside the kitchen. This time it is the poor man dragging his crutch, the unmistakable enemy, the hereditary enemy, the direct descendant of him who roamed outside the bone-cramped cave which you suddenly see again in your racial memory. Drunk with indignation, your bark broken, your teeth multiplied with hatred and rage, you are about to seize their reconcilable adversary by the breeches, when the cook, armed with her broom, the ancillary and forsworn sceptre, comes to protect the traitor, and you are obliged to go back to your hole, where, with eyes filled with impotent and slanting flames, you growl out frightful, but futile curses, thinking within yourself that this is the end of all things, and that the human species has lost its notion of justice and injustice....

Is that all? Not yet; for the smallest life is made up of innumerous duties, and it is a long work to organize a happy existence upon the borderland of two such different worlds as the world of beasts and the world of men. How should we fare if we had to serve, while remaining within our own sphere, a divinity, not an imaginary one, like to ourselves, because the offspring of our own brain, but a god actually visible, ever present, ever active and as foreign, as superior to our being as we are to the dog?

We now, to return to Pelléas, know pretty well what to do and how to behave on the master's premises. But the world does not end at the house-door, and, beyond the walls and beyond the hedge, there is a universe of which one has not the custody, where one is no longer at home, where relations are changed. How are we to stand in the street, in the fields, in the market-place, in the shops? In consequence of difficult and delicate observations, we understand that we must take no notice of passers-by; obey no calls but the master's; be polite, with indifference, to strangers who pet us. Next, we must conscientiously fulfil certain obligations of mysterious courtesy toward our brothers the other dogs; respect chickens and ducks; not appear to remark the cakes at the pastry-cook's, which spread themselves insolently within reach of the tongue; show to the cats, who, on the steps of the houses, provoke us by hideous grimaces, a silent contempt, but one that will not forget; and remember that it is lawful and even commendable to chase and strangle mice, rats, wild rabbits and, generally speaking, all animals (we learn to know them by secret marks) that have not yet made their peace with mankind.

All this and so much more!...Was it surprising that Pelléas often appeared pensive in the face of those numberless problems, and that his humble and gentle look was often so profound and grave, laden with cares and full of unreadable questions?

Alas, he did not have time to finish the long and heavy task which nature lays upon the instinct that rises in order to approach a brighter region....An ill of a mysterious character, which seems specially to punish the only animal that succeeds in leaving the circle in which it is born; an indefinite ill that carries off hundreds of intelligent little dogs, came to put an end to the destiny and the happy education of Pelléas. And now all those efforts to achieve a little more light; all that ardour in loving, that courage in understanding; all that affectionate gaiety and innocent fawning; all those kind and devoted looks, which turned to man to ask for his assistance against unjust death; all those flickering gleams which came from the profound abyss of a world that is no longer ours; all those nearly human little habits lie sadly in the cold ground, under a flowering elder-tree, in a corner of the garden.

II

Man loves the dog, but how much more ought he to love it if he considered, in the inflexible harmony of the laws of nature, the sole exception, which is that love of a being that succeeds in piercing, in order to draw closer to us, the partitions, every elsewhere impermeable, that separate the species! We are alone, absolutely alone on this chance planet; and amid all the forms of life that surround us, not one, excepting the dog, has made an alliance with us. A few creatures fear us, most are unaware of us, and not one loves us. In the world of plants, we have dumb and motionless slaves; but they serve us in spite of themselves. They simply endure our laws and our yoke. They are impotent prisoners, victims incapable of escaping, but silently rebellious; and, so soon as we lose sight of them, they hasten to betray us and return to their former wild and mischievous liberty. The rose and the corn, had they wings, would fly at our approach like the birds.

Among the animals, we number a few servants who have submitted only through indifference, cowardice or stupidity: the uncertain and craven horse, who responds only to pain and is attached to nothing; the passive and dejected ass, who stays with us only because he knows not what to do nor where to go, but who nevertheless, under the cudgel and the pack-saddle, retains the idea that lurks behind his ears; the cow and the ox, happy so long as they are eating, and docile because, for centuries, they have not had a thought of their own; the affrighted sheep, who knows no other master than terror; the hen, who is faithful to the poultry-yard because she finds more maize and wheat there than in the neighbouring forest. I do not speak of the cat, to whom we are nothing more than a too large and uneatable prey: the ferocious cat, whose sidelong contempt tolerates us only as encumbering parasites in our own homes. She, at least, curses us in her mysterious heart; but all the others live beside us as they might live beside a rock or a tree. They do not love us, do not know us, scarcely notice us. They are unaware of our life, our death, our departure, our return, our sadness, our joy, our smile. They do not even hear the sound of our voice, so soon as it no longer threatens them; and, when they look at us, it is with the distrustful bewilderment of the horse, in whose eye still hovers the infatuation of the elk or gazelle that sees us for the first time, or with the dull stupor of the ruminants, who look upon us as a momentary and useless accident of the pasture.

For thousands of years, they have been living at our side, as foreign to our thoughts, our affections, our habits as though the least fraternal of the stars had dropped them but yesterday on our globe. In the boundless interval that separates man from all the other creatures, we have succeeded only, by dint of patience, in making them take two or three illusory steps. And if, to-morrow, leaving their feelings toward us untouched, nature were to give them the intelligence and the weapons wherewith to conquer us, I confess that I should distrust the hasty vengeance of the horse, the obstinate reprisals of the ass and the maddened meekness of the sheep. I should shun the cat as I should shun the tiger; and even the good cow, solemn and somnolent, would inspire me with but a wary confidence. As for the hen, with her round, quick eye, as when discovering a slug or a worm, I am sure that she would devour me without a thought.

III

Now, in this indifference and this total want of comprehension in which everything that surrounds us lives; in this incommunicable world, where everything has its object hermetically contained within itself, where every destiny is self-circumscribed, where there exist among the creatures no other relations than those of executioners and victims, eaters and eaten, where nothing is able to leave its steel-bound sphere, where death alone establishes cruel relations of cause and effect between neighbouring lives, where not the smallest sympathy has ever made a conscious leap from one species to another, one animal alone, among all that breathes upon the earth, has succeeded in breaking through the prophetic circle, in escaping from itself to come bounding toward us, definitely to cross the enormous zone of darkness, ice and silence that isolates each category of existence in nature's unintelligible plan. This animal, our good familiar dog, simple and unsurprising as may to-day appear to us what he has done, in thus perceptibly drawing nearer to a world in which he was not born and for which he was not destined, has nevertheless performed one of the most unusual and improbable acts that we can find in the general history of life. When was this recognition of man by beast, this extraordinary passage from darkness to light, effected? Did we seek out the poodle, the collie, or the mastiff from among the wolves and the jackals, or did he come spontaneously to us? We cannot tell. So far as our human annals stretch, he is at our side, as at present; but what are human annals in comparison with the times of which we have no witness? The fact remains that he is there in our houses, as ancient, as rightly placed, as perfectly adapted to our habits as though he had appeared on this earth, such as he now is, at the same time as ourselves. We have not to gain his confidence or his friendship: he is born our friend; while his eyes are still closed, already he believes in us: even before his birth, he has given himself to man. But the word "friend" does not exactly depict his affectionate worship. He loves us and reveres us as though we had drawn him out of nothing. He is, before all, our creature full of gratitude and more devoted than the apple of our eye. He is our intimate and impassioned slave, whom nothing discourages, whom nothing repels, whose ardent trust and love nothing can impair. He has solved, in an admirable and touching manner, the terrifying problem which human wisdom would have to solve if a divine race came to occupy our globe. He has loyally, religiously, irrevocably recognized man's superiority and has surrendered himself to him body and soul, without after-thought, without any intention to go back, reserving of his independence, his instinct and his character only the small part indispensable to the continuation of the life prescribed by nature. With an unquestioning certainty, an unconstraint and a simplicity that surprise us a little, deeming us better and more powerful than all that exists, he betrays, for our benefit, the whole of the animal kingdom to which he belongs and, without scruple, denies his race, his kin, his mother and his young.

But he loves us not only in his consciousness and his intelligence: the very instinct of his race, the entire unconsciousness of his species, it appears, think only of us, dream only of being useful to us. To serve us better, to adapt himself better to our different needs, he has adopted every shape and been able infinitely to vary the faculties, the aptitudes which he places at our disposal. Is he to aid us in the pursuit of game in the plains? His legs lengthen inordinately, his muzzle tapers, his lungs widen, he becomes swifter than the deer. Does our prey hide under wood? The docile genius of the species, forestalling our desires, presents us with the basset, a sort of almost footless serpent, which steals into the closest thickets. Do we ask that he should drive our flocks? The same compliant genius grants him the requisite size, intelligence, energy and vigilance. Do we intend him to watch and defend our house? His head becomes round and monstrous, in order that his jaws may be more powerful, more formidable and more tenacious. Are we taking him to the south? His hair grows shorter and lighter, so that he may faithfully accompany us under the rays of a hotter sun. Are we going up to the north? His feet grow larger, the better to tread the snow; his fur thickens, in order that the cold may not compel him to abandon us. Is he intended only for us to play with, to amuse the leisure of our eyes, to adorn or enliven the home? He clothes himself in a sovereign grace and elegance, he makes himself smaller than a doll to sleep on our knees by the fireside, or even consents, should our fancy demand it, to appear a little ridiculous to please us.

You shall not find, in nature's immense crucible, a single living being that has shown a like suppleness, a similar abundance of forms, the same prodigious faculty of accommodation to our wishes. This is because, in the world which we know, among the different and primitive geniuses that preside over the evolution of the several species, there exists not one, excepting that of the dog, that ever gave a thought to the presence of man.

It will, perhaps, be said that we have been able to transform almost as profoundly some of our domestic animals: our hens, our pigeons, our ducks, our cats, our horses, our rabbits, for instance. Yes, perhaps; although such transformations are not comparable with those undergone by the dog and although the kind of service which these animals render us remains, so to speak, invariable. In any case, whether this impression be purely imaginary or correspond with a reality, it does not appear that we feel in these transformations the same unfailing and preventing good will, the same sagacious and exclusive love. For the rest, it is quite possible that the dog, or rather the inaccessible genius of his race, troubles scarcely at all about us and that we have merely known how to make use of various aptitudes offered by the abundant chances of life. It matters not: as we know nothing of the substance of things, we must needs cling to appearances; and it is sweet to establish that, at least in appearance, there is on the planet where, like unacknowledged kings, we live in solitary state, a being that loves us.

However the case may stand with these appearances, it is none the less certain that, in the aggregate of intelligent creatures that have rights, duties, a mission and a destiny, the dog is a really privileged animal. He occupies in this world a pre-eminent position enviable among all. He is the only living being that has found and recognizes an indubitable, tangible, unexceptional and definite god. He knows to what to devote the best part of himself. He knows to whom above him to give himself. He has not to seek for a perfect, superior and infinite power in the darkness, amid successive lies, hypotheses and dreams. That power is there, before him, and he moves in its light. He knows the supreme duties which we all do not know. He has a morality which surpasses all that he is able to discover in himself and which he can practise without scruple and without fear. He possesses truth in its fulness. He has a certain and infinite ideal.

IV

And it was thus that, the other day, before his illness, I saw my little Pelléas sitting at the foot of my writing-table, his tail carefully folded under his paws, his head a little on one side, the better to question me, at once attentive and tranquil, as a saint should be in the presence of God. He was happy with the happiness which we, perhaps, shall never know, since it sprang from the smile and the approval of a life incomparably higher than his own. He was there, studying, drinking in all my looks; and he replied to them gravely, as from equal to equal, to inform me, no doubt, that, at least through the eyes the most immaterial organ that transformed into affectionate intelligence the light which we enjoyed, he knew that he was saying to me all that love should say. And, when I saw him thus, young, ardent and believing, bringing me, in some wise, from the depths of unwearied nature, quite fresh news of life and trusting and wonderstruck, as though he had been the first of his race that came to inaugurate the earth and as though we were still in the first days of the world's existence, I envied the gladness of his certainty, compared it with the destiny of man, still plunging on every side into darkness, and said to myself that the dog who meets with a good master is the happier of the two.

A Yellow Dog
Bret Harte

I never knew why in the Western States of America a yellow dog should be proverbially considered the acme of canine degradation and incompetency, nor why the possession of one should seriously affect the social standing of its possessor. But the fact being established, I think we accepted it at Rattlers Ridge without question. The matter of ownership was more difficult to settle; and although the dog I have in my mind at the present writing attached himself impartially and equally to everyone in camp, no one ventured to exclusively claim him; while, after the perpetration of any canine atrocity, everybody repudiated him with indecent haste.

"Well, I can swear he hasn't been near our shanty for weeks," or the retort, "He was last seen comin' out of *your* cabin," expressed the eagerness with which Rattlers Ridge washed its hands of any responsibility. Yet he was by no means a common dog, nor even an unhandsome dog; and it was a singular fact that his severest critics vied with each other in narrating instances of his sagacity, insight, and agility which they themselves had witnessed.

He had been seen crossing the "flume" that spanned Grizzly Canyon at a height of nine hundred feet, on a plank six inches wide. He had tumbled down the "shoot" to the South Fork, a thousand feet below, and was found sitting on the riverbank "without a scratch, 'cept that he was lazily givin' himself with his off hind paw." He had been forgotten in a snowdrift on a Sierran shelf, and had come home in the early spring with the conceited complacency of an Alpine traveler and a plumpness alleged to have been the result of an exclusive diet of buried mail bags and their contents. He was generally believed to read the advance election posters, and disappear a day or two before the candidates and the brass band—which he hated—came to the Ridge. He was suspected of having overlooked Colonel Johnson's hand at poker, and of having conveyed to the Colonel's adversary, by a succession of barks, the danger of betting against four kings.

While these statements were supplied by wholly unsupported witnesses, it was a very human weakness of Rattlers Ridge that the responsibility of corroboration was passed to the dog himself, and *he* was looked upon as a consummate liar.

"Snoopin' round yere, and *callin'* yourself a poker sharp, are ye! Scoot, you yaller pizin!" was a common adjuration whenever the unfortunate animal intruded upon a card party. "Ef thar was a spark, an *atom* of truth in *that dog*, I'd believe my own eyes that I saw him sittin' up and trying to magnetize a jay bird off a tree. But wot are ye goin' to do with a yaller equivocator like that?"

I have said that he was yellow—or, to use the ordinary expression, "yaller." Indeed, I am inclined to believe that much of the ignominy attached to the epithet lay in this favorite pronunciation. Men who habitually spoke of a "*yellow* bird," a "*yellow*-hammer," a "*yellow* leaf," always alluded to him as a "*yaller* dog."

He certainly *was* yellow. After a bath—usually compulsory—he presented a decided gamboge streak down his back, from the top of his forehead to the stump of his tail, fading in his sides and flank to a delicate straw color. His breast, legs, and feet—when not reddened by "slumgullion," in which he was fond of wading—were white. A few attempts at ornamental decoration from the India-ink pot of the storekeeper failed, partly through the yellow dog's excessive agility, which would never give the paint time to dry on him, and partly through his success in transferring his markings to the trousers and blankets of the camp.

The size and shape of his tail—which had been cut off before his introduction to Rattlers Ridge—were favorite sources of speculation to the miners, as determining both his breed and his moral responsibility in coming into camp in that defective condition. There was a general opinion that he couldn't have looked worse with a tail, and its removal was therefore a gratuitous effrontery.

His best feature was his eyes, which were a lustrous Vandyke brown, and sparkling with intelligence; but here again he suffered from evolution through environment, and their original trustful openness was marred by the experience of watching for flying stones, sods, and passing kicks from the rear, so that the pupils were continually reverting to the outer angle of the eyelid.

Nevertheless, none of these characteristics decided the vexed question of his *breed*. His speed and scent pointed to a "hound," and it is related that on one occasion he was laid on the trail of a wildcat with such success that he followed it apparently out of the State, returning at the end of two weeks footsore, but blandly contented.

Attaching himself to a prospecting party, he was sent under the same belief, "into the brush" to drive off a bear, who was supposed to be haunting the campfire. He returned in a few minutes *with* the bear, *driving it into* the unarmed circle and scattering the whole party. After this the theory of his being a hunting dog was abandoned. Yet it was said—on the usual uncorroborated evidence—that he had "put up" a quail; and his qualities as a retriever were for a long time accepted, until, during a shooting expedition for wild ducks, it was discovered that the one he had brought back had never been shot, and the party were obliged to compound damages with an adjacent settler.

His fondness for paddling in the ditches and "slumgullion" at one time suggested a water spaniel. He could swim, and would occasionally bring out of the river sticks and pieces of bark that had been thrown in; but as *he* always had to be thrown in with them, and was a good-sized dog, his aquatic reputation faded also. He remained simply "a yaller dog." What more could be said? His actual name was "Bones"—given to him, no doubt, through the provincial custom of confounding the occupation of the individual with his quality, for which it was pointed out precedent could be found in some old English family names.

But if Bones generally exhibited no preference for any particular individual in camp, he always made an exception in favor of drunkards. Even an ordinary roistering bacchanalian party brought him out from under a tree or a shed in the keenest satisfaction. He would accompany them through the long straggling street of the settlement, barking his delight at every step or misstep of the revelers, and exhibiting none of that mistrust of eye which marked his attendance upon the sane and the respectable. He accepted even their uncouth play without a snarl or a yelp, hypocritically pretending even to like it; and I conscientiously believe would have allowed a tin can to be attached to his tail if the hand that tied it on were only unsteady, and the voice that bade him "lie still" were husky with liquor. He would "see" the party cheerfully into a saloon, wait outside the door—his tongue fairly lolling from his mouth in enjoyment—until they reappeared, permit them even to tumble over him with pleasure, and then gambol away before them, heedless of awkwardly projected stones and epithets. He would afterward accompany them separately home, or lie with them at crossroads until they were assisted to their cabins. Then he would trot rakishly to his own haunt by the saloon stove, with the slightly conscious air of having been a bad dog, yet of having had a good time.

We never could satisfy ourselves whether his enjoyment arose from some merely selfish conviction that he was more *secure* with the physically and mentally incompetent, from some active sympathy with active wickedness, or from a grim sense of his own mental superiority at such moments. But the general belief leant toward his kindred sympathy as a "yaller dog" with all that was disreputable. And this was supported by another very singular canine manifestation—the "sincere flattery" of simulation or imitation.

"Uncle Billy" Riley for a short time enjoyed the position of being the camp drunkard, and at once became an object of Bones' greatest solicitude. He not only accompanied him everywhere, curled at his feet or head according to Uncle Billy's attitude at the moment, but, it was noticed, began presently to undergo a singular alteration in his own habits and appearance. From being an active, tireless scout and forager, a bold and unovertakable marauder, he became lazy and apathetic; allowed gophers to burrow under him without endeavoring to undermine the settlement in his frantic endeavors to dig them out, permitted squirrels to flash their tails at him a hundred yards away, forgot his usual caches, and left his favorite bones unburied and bleaching in the sun. His eyes grew dull, his coat lusterless, in proportion as his companion became blear-eyed and ragged; in running, his usual arrowlike directness began to deviate, and it was not unusual to meet the pair together, zigzagging up the hill. Indeed, Uncle Billy's condition could be predetermined by Bones' appearance at times when his temporary master was invisible. "The old man must have an awful jag on today," was casually remarked when an extra fluffiness and imbecility was noticeable in the passing Bones. At first it was believed that he drank also, but when careful investigation proved this hypothesis untenable, he was freely called a "derned time-servin', yaller hypocrite." Not a few advanced the opinion that if Bones did not actually lead Uncle Billy astray, he at least "slavered him over and coddled him until the old man got conceited in his wickedness." This undoubtedly led to a compulsory divorce between them, and Uncle Billy was happily dispatched to a neighboring town and a doctor.

Bones seemed to miss him greatly, ran away for two days, and was supposed to have visited him, to have been shocked at his convalescence, and to have been "cut" by Uncle Billy in his reformed character; and he returned to his old active life again, and buried his past with his forgotten bones. It was said that he was afterward detected in trying to lead an intoxicated tramp into camp after the methods employed by a blind man's dog, but was discovered in time by the—of course—uncorroborated narrator.

I should be tempted to leave him thus in his original and picturesque sin, but the same veracity which compelled me to transcribe his faults and iniquities obliges me to describe his ultimate and somewhat monotonous reformation, which came from no fault of his own.

It was a joyous day at Rattlers Ridge that was equally the advent of his change of heart and the first stagecoach that had been induced to diverge from the highroad and stop regularly at our settlement. Flags were flying from the post office and Polka saloon, and Bones was flying before the brass band that he detested, when the sweetest girl in the county—Pinkey Preston—daughter of the county judge and hopelessly beloved by all Rattlers Ridge, stepped from the coach which she had glorified by occupying as an invited guest.

"What makes him run away?" she asked quickly, opening her lovely eyes in a possibly innocent wonder that anything could be found to run away from her.

"He don't like the brass band," we explained eagerly.

"How funny," murmured the girl; "is it as out of tune as all that?"

This irresistible witticism alone would have been enough to satisfy us—we did nothing but repeat it to each other all the next day—but we were positively transported when we saw her suddenly gather her dainty skirts in one hand and trip off through the red dust toward Bones, who, with his eyes over his yellow shoulder, had halted in the road, and half-turned in mingled disgust and rage at the spectacle of the descending trombone. We held our breath as she approached him. Would Bones evade her as he did us at such moments, or would he save our reputation, and consent, for the moment, to accept her as a new kind of inebriate? She came nearer; he saw her; he began to slowly quiver with excitement—his stump of a tail vibrating with such rapidity that the loss of the missing portion was scarcely noticeable. Suddenly she stopped before him, took his yellow head between her little hands, lifted it, and looked down in his handsome brown eyes with her two lovely blue ones. What passed between them in that magnetic glance no one ever knew. She returned with him; said to him casually: "We're not afraid of brass bands, are we?" to which he apparently acquiesced, at least stifling his disgust of them while he was near her—which was nearly all the time.

During the speechmaking her gloved hand and his yellow head were always near together, and at the crowning ceremony—her public checking of Yuba Bill's "waybill" on behalf of the township, with a gold pencil presented to her by the Stage Company—Bones' joy, far from knowing no bounds, seemed to know nothing but them, and he witnessed it apparently in the air. No one dared to interfere. For the first time a local pride in Bones sprang up in our hearts—and we lied to each other in his praises openly and shamelessly. Then the time came for parting. We were standing by the door of the coach, hats in hand, as Miss Pinkey was about to step into it; Bones was waiting by her side, confidently looking into the interior, and apparently selecting his own seat on the lap of Judge Preston in the corner, when Miss Pinkey held up the sweetest of admonitory fingers. Then, taking his head between her two hands, she again looked into his brimming eyes, and said, simply, "*good* dog," with the gentlest of emphasis on the adjective, and popped into the coach.

The six bay horses started as one, the gorgeous green and gold vehicle bounded forward, the red dust rose behind, and the yellow dog danced in and out of it to the very outskirts of the settlement. And then he soberly returned.

A day or two later he was missed—but the fact was afterward known that he was at Spring Valley, the county town where Miss Preston lived, and he was forgiven. A week afterward he was missed again, but this time for a longer period, and then a pathetic letter arrived from Sacramento for the storekeeper's wife.

"Would you mind," wrote Miss Pinkey Preston, "asking some of your boys to come over here to Sacramento and bring back Bones? I don't mind having the dear dog walk out with me at Spring Valley, where everyone knows me; but here he *does* make one so noticeable, on account of *his color*. I've got scarcely a frock that he agrees with. He don't go with my pink muslin, and that lovely buff tint he makes three shades lighter. You know yellow is *so* trying."

A consultation was quickly held by the whole settlement, and a deputation sent to Sacramento to relieve the unfortunate girl. We were all quite indignant with Bones—but, oddly enough, I think it

A Yellow Dog

was greatly tempered with our new pride in him. While he was with us alone, his peculiarities had been scarcely appreciated, but the recurrent phrase "that yellow dog that they keep at the Rattlers" gave us a mysterious importance along the countryside, as if we had secured a "mascot" in some zoological curiosity.

This was further indicated by a singular occurrence. A new church had been built at the crossroads, and an eminent divine had come from San Francisco to preach the opening sermon. After a careful examination of the camp's wardrobe, and some felicitous exchange of apparel, a few of us were deputed to represent "Rattlers" at the Sunday service. In our white ducks, straw hats, and flannel blouses, we were sufficiently picturesque and distinctive as "honest miners" to be shown off in one of the front pews.

Seated near the prettiest girls, who offered us their hymn books—in the cleanly odor of fresh pine shavings, and ironed muslin, and blown over by the spices of our own woods through the open windows, a deep sense of the abiding peace of Christian communion settled upon us. At this supreme moment someone murmured in an awe-stricken whisper:

"*Will* you look at Bones?"

We looked. Bones had entered the church and gone up in the gallery through a pardonable ignorance and modesty; but, perceiving his mistake, was now calmly walking along the gallery rail before the astounded worshippers. Reaching the end, he paused for a moment, and carelessly looked down. It was about fifteen feet to the floor below—the simplest jump in the world for the mountain-bred Bones. Daintily, gingerly, lazily, and yet with a conceited airiness of manner, as if, humanly speaking, he had one leg in his pocket and were doing it on three, he cleared the distance, dropping just in front of the chancel, without a sound, turned himself around three times, and then lay comfortably down.

Three deacons were instantly in the aisle, coming up before the eminent divine, who, we fancied, wore a restrained smile. We heard the hurried whispers: "Belongs to them." "Quite a local institution here, you know." "Don't like to offend sensibilities;" and the minister's prompt "By no means," as he went on with his service.

A short month ago we would have repudiated Bones; today we sat there in slightly supercilious attitudes, as if to indicate that any affront offered to Bones would be an insult to ourselves, and followed by our instantaneous withdrawal in a body.

All went well, however, until the minister, lifting the large Bible from the communion table and holding it in both hands before him, walked toward a reading stand by the altar rails. Bones uttered a distinct growl. The minister stopped.

We, and we alone, comprehended in a flash the whole situation. The Bible was nearly the size and shape of one of those soft clods of sod which we were in the playful habit of launching at Bones when he lay half-asleep in the sun, in order to see him cleverly evade it.

We held our breath. What was to be done? But the opportunity belonged to our leader, Jeff Briggs—a confoundedly good-looking fellow, with the golden mustache of a northern viking and the curls of an Apollo. Secure in his beauty and bland in his self-conceit, he rose from the pew, and stepped before the chancel rails.

"I would wait a moment, if I were you, sir," he said, respectfully, "and you will see that he will go out quietly."

"What is wrong?" whispered the minister in some concern.

"He thinks you are going to heave that book at him, sir, without giving him a fair show, as we do."

The minister looked perplexed, but remained motionless, with the book in his hands. Bones arose, walked halfway down the aisle, and vanished like a yellow flash!

A Yellow Dog

With this justification of his reputation, Bones disappeared for a week. At the end of that time we received a polite note from Judge Preston, saying that the dog had become quite domiciled in their house, and begged that the camp, without yielding up their valuable *property* in him, would allow him to remain at Spring Valley for an indefinite time; that both the judge and his daughter—with whom Bones was already an old friend—would be glad if the members of the camp would visit their old favorite whenever they desired, to assure themselves that he was well cared for.

I am afraid that the bait thus ingenuously thrown out had a good deal to do with our ultimate yielding. However, the reports of those who visited Bones were wonderful and marvelous. He was residing there in state, lying on rugs in the drawing-room, coiled up under the judicial desk in the judge's study, sleeping regularly on the mat outside Miss Pinkey's bedroom door, or lazily snapping at flies on the judge's lawn.

"He's as yaller as ever," said one of our informants, "but it don't somehow seem to be the same back that we used to break clods over in the old time, just to see him scoot out of the dust."

And now I must record a fact which I am aware all lovers of dogs will indignantly deny, and which will be furiously bayed at by every faithful hound since the days of Ulysses. Bones not only *forgot*, but absolutely *cut us*! Those who called upon the judge in "store clothes" he would perhaps casually notice, but he would sniff at them as if detecting and resenting them under their superficial exterior. The rest he simply paid no attention to. The more familiar term of "Bonesy"—formerly applied to him, as in our rare moments of endearment—produced no response. This pained, I think, some of the more youthful of us; but, through some strange human weakness, it also increased the camp's respect for him. Nevertheless, we spoke of him familiarly to strangers at the very moment he ignored us. I am afraid that we also took some pains to point out that he was getting fat and unwieldy, and losing his elasticity, implying covertly that his choice was a mistake and his life a failure.

A year after, he died, in the odor of sanctity and respectability, being found one morning coiled up and stiff on the mat outside Miss Pinkey's door. When the news was conveyed to us, we asked permission, the camp being in a prosperous condition, to erect a stone over his grave. But when it came to the inscription we could only think of the two words murmured to him by Miss Pinkey, which we always believe effected his conversion:

"*Good* Dog!"

The Lady with the Dog
Anton Chekhov

I

It was said that a new person had appeared on the sea-front: a lady with a little dog. Dmitri Dmitritch Gurov, who had by then been a fortnight at Yalta, and so was fairly at home there, had begun to take an interest in new arrivals. Sitting in Verney's pavilion, he saw, walking on the sea-front, a fair-haired young lady of medium height, wearing a beret; a white Pomeranian dog was running behind her.

And afterwards he met her in the public gardens and in the square several times a day. She was walking alone, always wearing the same beret, and always with the same white dog; no one knew who she was, and every one called her simply "the lady with the dog."

"If she is here alone without a husband or friends, it wouldn't be amiss to make her acquaintance," Gurov reflected.

He was under forty, but he had a daughter already twelve years old, and two sons at school. He had been married young, when he was a student in his second year, and by now his wife seemed half as old again as he. She was a tall, erect woman with dark eyebrows, staid and dignified, and, as she said of herself, intellectual. She read a great deal, used phonetic spelling, called her husband, not Dmitri, but Dimitri, and he secretly considered her unintelligent, narrow, inelegant, was afraid of her, and did not like to be at home. He had begun being unfaithful to her long ago—had been unfaithful to her often, and, probably on that account, almost always spoke ill of women, and when they were talked about in his presence, used to call them "the lower race."

It seemed to him that he had been so schooled by bitter experience that he might call them what he liked, and yet he could not get on for two days together without "the lower race." In the society of men he was bored and not himself, with them he was cold and uncommunicative; but when he was in the company of women he felt free, and knew what to say to them and how to behave; and he was at ease with them even when he was silent. In his appearance, in his character, in his whole nature, there was something attractive and elusive which allured women and disposed them in his favour; he knew that, and some force seemed to draw him, too, to them.

Experience often repeated, truly bitter experience, had taught him long ago that with decent people, especially Moscow people— always slow to move and irresolute—every intimacy, which at first so agreeably diversifies life and appears a light and charming adventure, inevitably grows into a regular problem of extreme intricacy, and in the long run the situation becomes unbearable. But at every fresh meeting with an interesting woman this experience seemed to slip out of his memory, and he was eager for life, and everything seemed simple and amusing.

One evening he was dining in the gardens, and the lady in the beret came up slowly to take the next table. Her expression, her gait, her dress, and the way she did her hair told him that she was a lady, that she was married, that she was in Yalta for the first time and alone, and that she was dull there....The stories told of the immorality in such places as Yalta are to a great extent untrue; he despised them, and knew that such stories were for the most part made up by persons who would themselves have been glad to sin if they had been able; but when the lady sat down at the next table three paces from him, he remembered these tales of easy conquests, of trips to the mountains, and the tempting thought of a swift, fleeting love affair, a romance with an unknown woman, whose name he did not know, suddenly took possession of him.

He beckoned coaxingly to the Pomeranian, and when the dog came up to him he shook his finger at it. The Pomeranian growled: Gurov shook his finger at it again.

The lady looked at him and at once dropped her eyes.

"He doesn't bite," she said, and blushed.

"May I give him a bone?" he asked; and when she nodded he asked courteously, "Have you been long in Yalta?"

"Five days."

"And I have already dragged out a fortnight here."

There was a brief silence.

"Time goes fast, and yet it is so dull here!" she said, not looking at him.

"That's only the fashion to say it is dull here. A provincial will live in Belyov or Zhidra and not be dull, and when he comes here it's 'Oh, the dulness! Oh, the dust!' One would think he came from Grenada."

She laughed. Then both continued eating in silence, like strangers, but after dinner they walked side by side; and there sprang up between them the light jesting conversation of people who are free and satisfied, to whom it does not matter where they go or what they talk about. They walked and talked of the strange light on the sea: the water was of a soft warm lilac hue, and there was a golden streak from the moon upon it. They talked of how sultry it was after a hot day. Gurov told her that he came from Moscow, that he had taken his degree in Arts, but had a post in a bank; that he had trained as an opera-singer, but had given it up, that he owned two houses in Moscow. ...And from her he learnt that she had grown up in Petersburg, but had lived in S---- since her marriage two years before, that she was staying another month in Yalta, and that her husband, who needed a holiday too, might perhaps come and fetch her. She was not sure whether her husband had a post in a Crown Department or under the Provincial Council—and was amused by her own ignorance. And Gurov learnt, too, that she was called Anna Sergeyevna.

Afterwards he thought about her in his room at the hotel— thought she would certainly meet him next day; it would be sure to happen. As he got into bed he thought how lately she had been a girl at school, doing lessons like his own daughter; he recalled the diffidence, the angularity, that was still manifest in her laugh and her manner of talking with a stranger. This must have been the first time in her life she had been alone in surroundings in which she was followed, looked at, and spoken to merely from a secret motive which she could hardly fail to guess. He recalled her slender, delicate neck, her lovely grey eyes.

"There's something pathetic about her, anyway," he thought, and fell asleep.

II

A week had passed since they had made acquaintance. It was a holiday. It was sultry indoors, while in the street the wind whirled the dust round and round, and blew people's hats off. It was a thirsty day, and Gurov often went into the pavilion, and pressed

Anna Sergeyevna to have syrup and water or an ice. One did not know what to do with oneself.

In the evening when the wind had dropped a little, they went out on the groyne to see the steamer come in. There were a great many people walking about the harbour; they had gathered to welcome some one, bringing bouquets. And two peculiarities of a well-dressed Yalta crowd were very conspicuous: the elderly ladies were dressed like young ones, and there were great numbers of generals.

Owing to the roughness of the sea, the steamer arrived late, after the sun had set, and it was a long time turning about before it reached the groyne. Anna Sergeyevna looked through her lorgnette at the steamer and the passengers as though looking for acquaintances, and when she turned to Gurov her eyes were shining. She talked a great deal and asked disconnected questions, forgetting next moment what she had asked; then she dropped her lorgnette in the crush.

The festive crowd began to disperse; it was too dark to see people's faces. The wind had completely dropped, but Gurov and Anna Sergeyevna still stood as though waiting to see some one else come from the steamer. Anna Sergeyevna was silent now, and sniffed the flowers without looking at Gurov.

"The weather is better this evening," he said. "Where shall we go now? Shall we drive somewhere?"

She made no answer.

Then he looked at her intently, and all at once put his arm round her and kissed her on the lips, and breathed in the moisture and the fragrance of the flowers; and he immediately looked round him, anxiously wondering whether any one had seen them.

"Let us go to your hotel," he said softly. And both walked quickly.

The room was close and smelt of the scent she had bought at the Japanese shop. Gurov looked at her and thought: "What different people one meets in the world!" From the past he preserved memories of careless, good-natured women, who loved cheerfully and were grateful to him for the happiness he gave them, however brief it might be; and of women like his wife who loved without any genuine feeling, with superfluous phrases, affectedly, hysterically, with an expression that suggested that it was not love nor passion, but something more significant; and of two or three others, very beautiful, cold women, on whose faces he had caught a glimpse of a rapacious expression—an obstinate desire to snatch from life more than it could give, and these were capricious, unreflecting, domineering, unintelligent women not in their first youth, and when Gurov grew cold to them their beauty excited his hatred, and the lace on their linen seemed to him like scales.

But in this case there was still the diffidence, the angularity of inexperienced youth, an awkward feeling; and there was a sense of consternation as though some one had suddenly knocked at the door. The attitude of Anna Sergeyevna—"the lady with the dog"—to what had happened was somehow peculiar, very grave, as though it were her fall—so it seemed, and it was strange and inappropriate. Her face dropped and faded, and on both sides of it her long hair hung down mournfully; she mused in a dejected attitude like "the woman who was a sinner" in an old-fashioned picture.

"It's wrong," she said. "You will be the first to despise me now."

There was a water-melon on the table. Gurov cut himself a slice and began eating it without haste. There followed at least half an hour of silence.

Anna Sergeyevna was touching; there was about her the purity of a good, simple woman who had seen little of life. The solitary candle burning on the table threw a faint light on her face, yet it was clear that she was very unhappy.

"How could I despise you?" asked Gurov. "You don't know what you are saying."

"God forgive me," she said, and her eyes filled with tears. "It's awful."

"You seem to feel you need to be forgiven."

"Forgiven? No. I am a bad, low woman; I despise myself and don't attempt to justify myself. It's not my husband but myself I have deceived. And not only just now; I have been deceiving myself for a long time. My husband may be a good, honest man, but he is a flunkey! I don't know what he does there, what his work is, but I know he is a flunkey! I was twenty when I was married to him. I have been tormented by curiosity; I wanted something better. 'There must be a different sort of life,' I said to myself. I wanted to live! To live, to live! ...I was fired by curiosity...you don't understand it, but, I swear to God, I could not control myself; something happened to me: I could not be restrained. I told my husband I was ill, and came here....And here I have been walking about as though I were dazed, like a mad creature; ...and now I have become a vulgar, contemptible woman whom any one may despise."

Gurov felt bored already, listening to her. He was irritated by the naive tone, by this remorse, so unexpected and inopportune; but for the tears in her eyes, he might have thought she was jesting or playing a part.

"I don't understand," he said softly. "What is it you want?"

She hid her face on his breast and pressed close to him.

"Believe me, believe me, I beseech you..." she said. "I love a pure, honest life, and sin is loathsome to me. I don't know what I am doing. Simple people say: 'The Evil One has beguiled me.' And I may say of myself now that the Evil One has beguiled me."

"Hush, hush!..." he muttered.

He looked at her fixed, scared eyes, kissed her, talked softly and affectionately, and by degrees she was comforted, and her gaiety returned; they both began laughing.

Afterwards when they went out there was not a soul on the sea-front. The town with its cypresses had quite a deathlike air, but the sea still broke noisily on the shore; a single barge was rocking on the waves, and a lantern was blinking sleepily on it.

They found a cab and drove to Oreanda.

"I found out your surname in the hall just now: it was written on the board—Von Diderits," said Gurov. "Is your husband a German?"

"No; I believe his grandfather was a German, but he is an Orthodox Russian himself."

At Oreanda they sat on a seat not far from the church, looked down at the sea, and were silent. Yalta was hardly visible through the morning mist; white clouds stood motionless on the mountain-tops. The leaves did not stir on the trees, grasshoppers chirruped, and the monotonous hollow sound of the sea rising up from below, spoke of the peace, of the eternal sleep awaiting us. So it must have sounded when there was no Yalta, no Oreanda here; so it sounds now, and it will sound as indifferently and monotonously when we are all no more. And in this constancy, in this complete indifference to the life and death of each of us, there lies hid, perhaps, a pledge of our eternal salvation, of the unceasing movement of life upon earth, of unceasing progress towards perfection. Sitting beside a young woman who in the dawn seemed so lovely, soothed and spellbound in these magical surroundings—the sea, mountains, clouds, the open sky—Gurov thought how in reality everything is beautiful in this world when one reflects: everything except what we think or do ourselves when we forget our human dignity and the higher aims of our existence.

The Lady with the Dog

A man walked up to them—probably a keeper—looked at them and walked away. And this detail seemed mysterious and beautiful, too. They saw a steamer come from Theodosia, with its lights out in the glow of dawn.

"There is dew on the grass," said Anna Sergeyevna, after a silence.

"Yes. It's time to go home."

They went back to the town.

Then they met every day at twelve o'clock on the sea-front, lunched and dined together, went for walks, admired the sea. She complained that she slept badly, that her heart throbbed violently; asked the same questions, troubled now by jealousy and now by the fear that he did not respect her sufficiently. And often in the square or gardens, when there was no one near them, he suddenly drew her to him and kissed her passionately. Complete idleness, these kisses in broad daylight while he looked round in dread of some one's seeing them, the heat, the smell of the sea, and the continual passing to and fro before him of idle, well-dressed, well-fed people, made a new man of him; he told Anna Sergeyevna how beautiful she was, how fascinating. He was impatiently passionate, he would not move a step away from her, while she was often pensive and continually urged him to confess that he did not respect her, did not love her in the least, and thought of her as nothing but a common woman. Rather late almost every evening they drove somewhere out of town, to Oreanda or to the waterfall; and the expedition was always a success, the scenery invariably impressed them as grand and beautiful.

They were expecting her husband to come, but a letter came from him, saying that there was something wrong with his eyes, and he entreated his wife to come home as quickly as possible. Anna Sergeyevna made haste to go.

"It's a good thing I am going away," she said to Gurov. "It's the finger of destiny!"

She went by coach and he went with her. They were driving the whole day. When she had got into a compartment of the express, and when the second bell had rung, she said:

"Let me look at you once more...look at you once again. That's right."

She did not shed tears, but was so sad that she seemed ill, and her face was quivering.

"I shall remember you...think of you," she said. "God be with you; be happy. Don't remember evil against me. We are parting forever—it must be so, for we ought never to have met. Well, God be with you."

The train moved off rapidly, its lights soon vanished from sight, and a minute later there was no sound of it, as though everything had conspired together to end as quickly as possible that sweet delirium, that madness. Left alone on the platform, and gazing into the dark distance, Gurov listened to the chirrup of the grasshoppers and the hum of the telegraph wires, feeling as though he had only just waked up. And he thought, musing, that there had been another episode or adventure in his life, and it, too, was at an end, and nothing was left of it but a memory. ...He was moved, sad, and conscious of a slight remorse. This young woman whom he would never meet again had not been happy with him; he was genuinely warm and affectionate with her, but yet in his manner, his tone, and his caresses there had been a shade of light irony, the coarse condescension of a happy man who was, besides, almost twice her age. All the time she had called him kind, exceptional, lofty; obviously he had seemed to her different from what he really was, so he had unintentionally deceived her....

Here at the station was already a scent of autumn; it was a cold evening.

"It's time for me to go north," thought Gurov as he left the platform.

"High time!"

III

At home in Moscow everything was in its winter routine; the stoves were heated, and in the morning it was still dark when the children were having breakfast and getting ready for school, and the nurse would light the lamp for a short time. The frosts had begun already. When the first snow has fallen, on the first day of sledge-driving it is pleasant to see the white earth, the white roofs, to draw soft, delicious breath, and the season brings back the days of one's youth. The old limes and birches, white with hoar-frost, have a good-natured expression; they are nearer to one's heart than cypresses and palms, and near them one doesn't want to be thinking of the sea and the mountains.

Gurov was Moscow born; he arrived in Moscow on a fine frosty day, and when he put on his fur coat and warm gloves, and walked along Petrovka, and when on Saturday evening he heard the ringing of the bells, his recent trip and the places he had seen lost all charm for him. Little by little he became absorbed in Moscow life, greedily read three newspapers a day, and declared he did not read the Moscow papers on principle! He already felt a longing to go to restaurants, clubs, dinner-parties, anniversary celebrations, and he felt flattered at entertaining distinguished lawyers and artists, and at playing cards with a professor at the doctors' club. He could already eat a whole plateful of salt fish and cabbage.

In another month, he fancied, the image of Anna Sergeyevna

would be shrouded in a mist in his memory, and only from time to time would visit him in his dreams with a touching smile as others did. But more than a month passed, real winter had come, and everything was still clear in his memory as though he had parted with Anna Sergeyevna only the day before. And his memories glowed more and more vividly. When in the evening stillness he heard from his study the voices of his children, preparing their lessons, or when he listened to a song or the organ at the restaurant, or the storm howled in the chimney, suddenly everything would rise up in his memory: what had happened on the groyne, and the early morning with the mist on the mountains, and the steamer coming from Theodosia, and the kisses. He would pace a long time about his room, remembering it all and smiling; then his memories passed into dreams, and in his fancy the past was mingled with what was to come. Anna Sergeyevna did not visit him in dreams, but followed him about everywhere like a shadow and haunted him. When he shut his eyes he saw her as though she were living before him, and she seemed to him lovelier, younger, tenderer than she was; and he imagined himself finer than he had been in Yalta. In the evenings she peeped out at him from the bookcase, from the fireplace, from the corner—he heard her breathing, the caressing rustle of her dress. In the street he watched the women, looking for some one like her.

He was tormented by an intense desire to confide his memories to some one. But in his home it was impossible to talk of his love, and he had no one outside; he could not talk to his tenants nor to any one at the bank. And what had he to talk of? Had he been in love, then? Had there been anything beautiful, poetical, or edifying or simply interesting in his relations with Anna Sergeyevna? And there was nothing for him but to talk vaguely of love, of woman, and no one guessed what it meant; only his wife twitched her black eyebrows, and said:

"The part of a lady-killer does not suit you at all, Dimitri."

One evening, coming out of the doctors' club with an official with whom he had been playing cards, he could not resist saying:

"If only you knew what a fascinating woman I made the acquaintance of in Yalta!"

The official got into his sledge and was driving away, but turned suddenly and shouted:

"Dmitri Dmitritch!"

"What?"

"You were right this evening: the sturgeon was a bit too strong!"

These words, so ordinary, for some reason moved Gurov to indignation, and struck him as degrading and unclean. What savage manners, what people! What senseless nights, what uninteresting, uneventful days! The rage for card-playing, the gluttony, the drunkenness, the continual talk always about the same thing. Useless pursuits and conversations always about the same things absorb the better part of one's time, the better part of one's strength, and in the end there is left a life grovelling and curtailed, worthless and trivial, and there is no escaping or getting away from it—just as though one were in a madhouse or a prison.

Gurov did not sleep all night, and was filled with indignation. And he had a headache all next day. And the next night he slept badly; he sat up in bed, thinking, or paced up and down his room. He was sick of his children, sick of the bank; he had no desire to go anywhere or to talk of anything.

In the holidays in December he prepared for a journey, and told his wife he was going to Petersburg to do something in the interests of a young friend—and he set off for S----. What for? He did not very well know himself. He wanted to see Anna Sergeyevna and to talk with her—to arrange a meeting, if possible.

He reached S---- in the morning, and took the best room at the hotel, in which the floor was covered with grey army cloth, and on the table was an inkstand, grey with dust and adorned with a figure on horseback, with its hat in its hand and its head broken off. The hotel porter gave him the necessary information; Von Diderits lived in a house of his own in Old Gontcharny Street—it was not far from the hotel: he was rich and lived in good style, and had his own horses; every one in the town knew him. The porter pronounced the name "Dridirits."

Gurov went without haste to Old Gontcharny Street and found the house. Just opposite the house stretched a long grey fence adorned with nails.

"One would run away from a fence like that," thought Gurov, looking from the fence to the windows of the house and back again.

He considered: to-day was a holiday, and the husband would probably be at home. And in any case it would be tactless to go into the house and upset her. If he were to send her a note it might fall into her husband's hands, and then it might ruin everything. The best thing was to trust to chance. And he kept walking up and down the street by the fence, waiting for the chance. He saw a beggar go in at the gate and dogs fly at him; then an hour later he heard a piano, and the sounds were faint and indistinct. Probably it was Anna Sergeyevna playing. The front door suddenly opened, and an old woman came out, followed by the familiar white Pomeranian. Gurov was on the point of calling to the dog, but his heart began beating violently, and in his excitement he could not remember the dog's name.

He walked up and down, and loathed the grey fence more and more, and by now he thought irritably that Anna Sergeyevna had forgotten him, and was perhaps already amusing herself with some one else, and that that was very natural in a young woman who had nothing to look at from morning till night but that confounded fence. He went back to his hotel room and sat for a long while on the sofa, not knowing what to do, then he had dinner and a long nap.

"How stupid and worrying it is!" he thought when he woke and looked at the dark windows: it was already evening. "Here I've had a good sleep for some reason. What shall I do in the night?"

He sat on the bed, which was covered by a cheap grey blanket, such as one sees in hospitals, and he taunted himself in his vexation:

"So much for the lady with the dog...so much for the adventure....You're in a nice fix...."

That morning at the station a poster in large letters had caught his eye. "The Geisha" was to be performed for the first time. He thought of this and went to the theatre.

"It's quite possible she may go to the first performance," he thought.

The theatre was full. As in all provincial theatres, there was a fog above the chandelier, the gallery was noisy and restless; in the front row the local dandies were standing up before the beginning of the performance, with their hands behind them; in the Governor's box the Governor's daughter, wearing a boa, was sitting in the front seat, while the Governor himself lurked modestly behind the curtain with only his hands visible; the orchestra was a long time tuning up; the stage curtain swayed. All the time the audience were coming in and taking their seats Gurov looked at them eagerly.

Anna Sergeyevna, too, came in. She sat down in the third row, and when Gurov looked at her his heart contracted, and he understood clearly that for him there was in the whole world no creature so near, so precious, and so important to him; she, this little woman, in no way remarkable, lost in a provincial crowd, with a vulgar lorgnette in her hand, filled his whole life now, was his sorrow and his joy, the one happiness that he now desired for himself, and to the sounds of the inferior orchestra, of the wretched provincial violins, he thought how lovely she was. He thought and dreamed.

A young man with small side-whiskers, tall and stooping, came in with Anna Sergeyevna and sat down beside her; he bent his head at every step and seemed to be continually bowing. Most likely this was the husband whom at Yalta, in a rush of bitter feeling, she had called a flunkey. And there really was in his long figure, his side-whiskers, and the small bald patch on his head, something of the flunkey's obsequiousness; his smile was sugary, and in his buttonhole there was some badge of distinction like the number on a waiter.

During the first interval the husband went away to smoke; she remained alone in her stall. Gurov, who was sitting in the stalls, too, went up to her and said in a trembling voice, with a forced smile:

"Good-evening."

She glanced at him and turned pale, then glanced again with horror, unable to believe her eyes, and tightly gripped the fan and the lorgnette in her hands, evidently struggling with herself not to faint. Both were silent. She was sitting, he was standing, frightened by her confusion and not venturing to sit down beside her. The violins and the flute began tuning up. He felt suddenly frightened; it seemed as though all the people in the boxes were looking at them. She got up and went quickly to the door; he followed her, and both walked senselessly along passages, and up and down stairs, and figures in legal, scholastic, and civil service uniforms, all wearing badges, flitted before their eyes. They caught glimpses of ladies, of fur coats hanging on pegs; the draughts blew on them, bringing a smell of stale tobacco. And Gurov, whose heart was beating violently, thought:

"Oh, heavens! Why are these people here and this orchestra!..."

And at that instant he recalled how when he had seen Anna Sergeyevna off at the station he had thought that everything was over and they would never meet again. But how far they were still from the end!

On the narrow, gloomy staircase over which was written "To the Amphitheatre," she stopped.

"How you have frightened me!" she said, breathing hard, still pale and overwhelmed. "Oh, how you have frightened me! I am half dead. Why have you come? Why?"

"But do understand, Anna, do understand..." he said hastily in a low voice. "I entreat you to understand...."

She looked at him with dread, with entreaty, with love; she looked at him intently, to keep his features more distinctly in her memory.

"I am so unhappy," she went on, not heeding him. "I have thought of nothing but you all the time; I live only in the thought of you. And I wanted to forget, to forget you; but why, oh, why, have you come?"

On the landing above them two schoolboys were smoking and looking down, but that was nothing to Gurov; he drew Anna Sergeyevna to him, and began kissing her face, her cheeks, and her hands.

"What are you doing, what are you doing!" she cried in horror, pushing him away. "We are mad. Go away to-day; go away at once.... I beseech you by all that is sacred, I implore you.... There are people coming this way!"

Some one was coming up the stairs.

"You must go away," Anna Sergeyevna went on in a whisper. "Do you hear, Dmitri Dmitritch? I will come and see you in Moscow. I have never been happy; I am miserable now, and I never,

never shall be happy, never! Don't make me suffer still more! I swear I'll come to Moscow. But now let us part. My precious, good, dear one, we must part!"

She pressed his hand and began rapidly going downstairs, looking round at him, and from her eyes he could see that she really was unhappy. Gurov stood for a little while, listened, then, when all sound had died away, he found his coat and left the theatre.

IV

And Anna Sergeyevna began coming to see him in Moscow. Once in two or three months she left S----, telling her husband that she was going to consult a doctor about an internal complaint—and her husband believed her, and did not believe her. In Moscow she stayed at the Slaviansky Bazaar hotel, and at once sent a man in a red cap to Gurov. Gurov went to see her, and no one in Moscow knew of it.

Once he was going to see her in this way on a winter morning (the messenger had come the evening before when he was out). With him walked his daughter, whom he wanted to take to school: it was on the way. Snow was falling in big wet flakes.

"It's three degrees above freezing-point, and yet it is snowing," said Gurov to his daughter. "The thaw is only on the surface of the earth; there is quite a different temperature at a greater height in the atmosphere."

"And why are there no thunderstorms in the winter, father?"

He explained that, too. He talked, thinking all the while that he was going to see her, and no living soul knew of it, and probably never would know. He had two lives: one, open, seen and known by all who cared to know, full of relative truth and of relative falsehood, exactly like the lives of his friends and acquaintances; and another life running its course in secret. And through some strange, perhaps accidental, conjunction of circumstances, everything that was essential, of interest and of value to him, everything in which he was sincere and did not deceive himself, everything that made the kernel of his life, was hidden from other people; and all that was false in him, the sheath in which he hid himself to conceal the truth—such, for instance, as his work in the bank, his discussions at the club, his "lower race," his presence with his wife at anniversary festivities—all that was open. And he judged of others by himself, not believing in what he saw, and always believing that every man had his real, most interesting life under the cover of secrecy and under the cover of night. All personal life rested on secrecy, and possibly it was partly on that account that civilised man was so nervously anxious that personal privacy should be respected.

After leaving his daughter at school, Gurov went on to the Slaviansky Bazaar. He took off his fur coat below, went upstairs, and softly knocked at the door. Anna Sergeyevna, wearing his favourite grey dress, exhausted by the journey and the suspense, had been expecting him since the evening before. She was pale; she looked at him, and did not smile, and he had hardly come in when she fell on his breast. Their kiss was slow and prolonged, as though they had not met for two years.

"Well, how are you getting on there?" he asked. "What news?"

"Wait; I'll tell you directly.... I can't talk."

She could not speak; she was crying. She turned away from him, and pressed her handkerchief to her eyes.

"Let her have her cry out. I'll sit down and wait," he thought, and he sat down in an arm-chair.

Then he rang and asked for tea to be brought him, and while he drank his tea she remained standing at the window with her back to him. She was crying from emotion, from the miserable consciousness that their life was so hard for them; they could only meet in secret, hiding themselves from people, like thieves! Was not their life shattered?

"Come, do stop!" he said.

It was evident to him that this love of theirs would not soon be over, that he could not see the end of it. Anna Sergeyevna grew more and more attached to him. She adored him, and it was unthinkable to say to her that it was bound to have an end some day; besides, she would not have believed it!

He went up to her and took her by the shoulders to say something affectionate and cheering, and at that moment he saw himself in the looking-glass.

His hair was already beginning to turn grey. And it seemed strange to him that he had grown so much older, so much plainer during the last few years. The shoulders on which his hands rested were warm and quivering. He felt compassion for this life, still so warm and lovely, but probably already not far from beginning to fade and wither like his own. Why did she love him so much? He always seemed to women different from what he was, and they loved in him not himself, but the man created by their imagination, whom they had been eagerly seeking all their lives; and afterwards, when they noticed their mistake, they loved him all the same. And not one of them had been happy with him. Time passed, he had made their acquaintance, got on with them, parted, but he had never once loved; it was anything you like, but not love.

And only now when his head was grey he had fallen properly, really in love—for the first time in his life.

Anna Sergeyevna and he loved each other like people very close and akin, like husband and wife, like tender friends; it seemed to them that fate itself had meant them for one another, and they could not understand why he had a wife and she a husband; and it was as though they were a pair of birds of passage, caught and forced to live in different cages. They forgave each other for what they were ashamed of in their past, they forgave everything in the present, and felt that this love of theirs had changed them both.

In moments of depression in the past he had comforted himself with any arguments that came into his mind, but now he no longer cared for arguments; he felt profound compassion, he wanted to be sincere and tender....

"Don't cry, my darling," he said. "You've had your cry; that's enough.... Let us talk now, let us think of some plan."

Then they spent a long while taking counsel together, talked of how to avoid the necessity for secrecy, for deception, for living in different towns and not seeing each other for long at a time. How could they be free from this intolerable bondage?

"How? How?" he asked, clutching his head. "How?"

And it seemed as though in a little while the solution would be found, and then a new and splendid life would begin; and it was clear to both of them that they had still a long, long road before them, and that the most complicated and difficult part of it was only just beginning.

Rab and His Friends
John Brown, M.D.

Four-and-thirty years ago, Bob Ainslie and I were coming up Infirmary Street from the High School, our heads together, and our arms intertwisted, as only lovers and boys know how, or why.

When we got to the top of the street, and turned north, we espied a crowd at the Tron Church. "A dog-fight!" shouted Bob, and was off; and so was I, both of us all but praying that it might not be over before we got up! And is not this boy-nature? and human nature too? and don't we all wish a house on fire not to be out before we see it? Dogs like fighting; old Isaac says they "delight" in it, and for the best of all reasons; and boys are not cruel because they like to see the fight. They see three of the great cardinal virtues of dog or man—courage, endurance, and skill—in intense action. This is very different from a love of making dogs fight, and enjoying, and aggravating, and making gain by their pluck. A boy,—be he ever so fond himself of fighting,—if he be a good boy, hates and despises all this, but he would have run off with Bob and me fast enough: it is a natural, and a not wicked interest, that all boys and men have in witnessing intense energy in action.

Does any curious and finely-ignorant woman wish to know how Bob's eye at a glance announced a dog-fight to his brain? He did not, he could not, see the dogs fighting: it was a flash of an inference, a rapid induction. The crowd round a couple of dogs fighting is a crowd masculine mainly, with an occasional active, compassionate woman fluttering wildly round the outside and using her tongue and her hands freely upon the men, as so many "brutes;" it is a crowd annular, compact, and mobile; a crowd centripetal, having its eyes and its heads all bent downwards and inwards, to one common focus.

Well, Bob and I are up, and find it is not over: a small thoroughbred white bull terrier is busy throttling a large shepherd's dog, unaccustomed to war, but not to be trifled with. They are hard at it; the scientific little fellow doing his work in great style, his pastoral enemy fighting wildly, but with the sharpest of teeth and a great courage. Science and breeding, however, soon had their own; the Game Chicken, as the premature Bob called him, working his way up, took his final grip of poor Yarrow's throat,—and he lay gasping and done for. His master, a brown, handsome, big young shepherd from Tweedsmuir, would have liked to have knocked down any man, would "drink up Esil, or eat a crocodile," for that part, if he had a chance: it was no use kicking the little dog; that would only make him hold the closer. Many were the means shouted out in mouthfuls, of the best possible ways of ending it. "Water!" but there was none near, and many cried for it who might have got it from the well at Blackfriar's Wynd. "Bite the tail!" and a large, vague, benevolent, middle-aged man, more desirous than wise, with some struggle got the bushy end of Yarrow's tail into his ample mouth, and bit it with all his might. This was more than enough for the much-enduring, much perspiring shepherd, who, with a gleam of joy over his broad visage, delivered a terrific facer upon our large, vague, benevolent, middle-aged friend, who went down like a shot.

Still the Chicken holds; death not far off. "Snuff! a pinch of snuff!" observed a calm, highly-dressed young buck, with an eyeglass in his eye. "Snuff, indeed!" growled the angry crowd, affronted and glaring. "Snuff! a pinch of snuff!" again observes the buck, but with more urgency; whereon were produced several open boxes, and from a mull which may have been at Culloden he took a pinch, knelt down, and presented it to the nose of the Chicken. The laws of physiology and of snuff take their course; the Chicken sneezes, and Yarrow is free!

The young pastoral giant stalks off with Yarrow in his arms, comforting him.

But the Bull Terrier's blood is up, and his soul unsatisfied; he grips the first dog he meets, and discovering she is not a dog, in Homeric phrase, he makes a brief sort of amende, and is off. The boys, with Bob and me at their head, are after him: down Niddry Street he goes, bent on mischief; up the Cowgate like an arrow— Bob and I, and our small men, panting behind.

There, under the single arch of the South Bridge, is a huge mastiff, sauntering down the middle of the causeway, as if with his hands in his pockets: he is old, gray, brindled, as big as a little Highland bull, and has the Shakespearian dewlaps shaking as he goes.

The Chicken makes straight at him, and fastens on his throat. To our astonishment the great creature does nothing but stand still, hold himself up, and roar—yes, roar; a long, serious, remonstrative roar. How is this? Bob and I are up to them. *He is muzzled!* The bailies had proclaimed a general muzzling, and his master, studying strength and economy mainly, had encompassed his huge jaws in a home-made apparatus constructed out of the leather of some ancient breechin. His mouth was open as far as it could; his lips curled up in rage, a sort of terrible grin; his teeth gleaming, ready, from out the darkness; the strap across his mouth tense as a bow-string; his whole frame stiff with indignation and surprise; his roar asking us all around, "Did you ever see the like of this?" He looked a statue of anger and astonishment done in Aberdeen granite.

We soon had a crowd: the Chicken held on. "A knife!" cried Bob; and a cobbler gave him his knife: you know the kind of knife, worn away obliquely to a point, and always keen. I put its edge to the tense leather; it ran before it; and then!—one sudden jerk of that enormous head, a sort of dirty mist about his mouth, no noise, and the bright and fierce little fellow is dropped, limp and dead. A solemn pause; this was more than any of us had bargained for. I turned the little fellow over, and saw he was quite dead; the mastiff had taken him by the small of the back like a rat, and broken it.

He looked down at his victim appeased, ashamed, and amazed, snuffed him all over, stared at him, and, taking a sudden thought, turned round and trotted off. Bob took the dead dog up, and said, "John, we'll bury him after tea." "Yes," said I, and was off after the mastiff. He made up the Cowgate at a rapid swing; he had forgotten some engagement. He turned up the Candlemaker Row, and stopped at the Harrow Inn.

There was a carrier's cart ready to start, and a keen, thin, impatient, black-a-vised little man, his hand at his gray horse's head, looking about angrily for something. "Rab, ye thief!" said he, aiming a kick at my great friend, who drew cringing up, and, avoiding the heavy shoe with more agility than dignity, and watching his master's eye, slunk dismayed under the cart, his ears down, and as much as he had of tail down too.

What a man this must be—thought I—to whom my tremendous hero turns tail! The carrier saw the muzzle hanging, cut and useless, from his neck, and I eagerly told him the story, which Bob and I always thought, and still think, Homer, or King David, or Sir Walter, alone were worthy to rehearse. The severe little man was mitigated, and condescended to say, "Rab, ma man, puir Rabbie!"—

whereupon the stump of a tail rose up, the ears were cocked, the eyes filled, and were comforted; the two friends were reconciled. "Hupp!" and a stroke of the whip were given to Jess; and off went the three.

Bob and I buried the Game Chicken that night (we had not much of a tea) in the back-green of his house, in Melville Street, No. 17, with considerable gravity and silence; and being at the time in the Iliad, and, like all boys, Trojans, we called him Hector, of course.

Six years have passed,—a long time for a boy and a dog: Bob Ainslie is off to the wars; I am a medical student, and clerk at Minto House Hospital. Rab I saw almost every week, on the Wednesday; and we had much pleasant intimacy. I found the way to his heart by frequent scratching of his huge head, and an occasional bone. When I did not notice him he would plant himself straight before me, and stand wagging that bud of a tail, and looking up, with his head a little to the one side. His master I occasionally saw; he used to call me "Maister John," but was laconic as any Spartan.

One fine October afternoon, I was leaving the hospital, when I saw the large gate open, and in walked Rab, with that great and easy saunter of his. He looked as if taking general possession of the place; like the Duke of Wellington entering a subdued city, satiated with victory and peace. After him came Jess, now white from age, with her cart, and in it a woman carefully wrapped up, the carrier leading the horse anxiously, and looking back. When he saw me, James (for his name was James Noble) made a curt and grotesque "boo," and said, "Maister John, this is the mistress; she's got a trouble in her breest—some kind o' an income, we're thinkin'."

By this time I saw the woman's face; she was sitting on a sack filled with straw, her husband's plaid round her, and his big-coat, with its large white metal buttons, over her feet.

I never saw a more unforgettable face—pale, serious, *lonely*,[1] delicate, sweet, without being at all what we call fine. She looked sixty, and had on a mutch, white as snow, with its black ribbon; her silvery, smooth hair setting off her dark-gray eyes,—eyes such as one sees only twice or thrice in a lifetime, full of suffering, full also of the overcoming of it; her eyebrows[2] black and delicate, and her mouth firm, patient, and contented, which few mouths ever are.

As I have said, I never saw a more beautiful countenance, or one more subdued to settled quiet. "Ailie," said James, "this is Maister John, the young doctor; Rab's freend, ye ken. We often speak aboot you, doctor." She smiled, and made a movement, but said nothing, and prepared to come down, putting her plaid aside and rising. Had Solomon, in all his glory, been handing down the Queen of Sheba at his palace gate, he could not have done it more daintily, more tenderly, more like a gentleman, than did James the Howgate carrier, when he lifted down Ailie his wife. The contrast of his small, swarthy, weather-beaten, keen, worldly face to hers—pale, subdued, and beautiful—was something wonderful. Rab looked on concerned and puzzled, but ready for anything that might turn up—were it to strangle the nurse, the porter, or even me. Ailie and he seemed great friends.

"As I was sayin', she's got a kind o' trouble in her breest, doctor: wull ye tak' a look at it?" We walked into the consulting-room, all four, Rab grim and comic, willing to be happy and confidential if cause could be shown, willing also to be the reverse on the same terms. Ailie sat down, undid her open gown and her lawn handkerchief round her neck, and, without a word, showed me her right breast. I looked at and examined it carefully,—she and James watching me, and Rab eying all three. What could I say? There it was, that had once been so soft, so shapely, so white, so gracious and bountiful, so "full of all blessed conditions,"—hard as a stone, a centre of horrid pain, making that pale face, with its gray, lucid, reasonable eyes, and its sweet resolved mouth, express the full measure of suffering overcome. Why was that gentle, modest, sweet woman, clean and lovable, condemned by God to bear such a burden?

I got her away to bed. "May Rab and me bide?" said James. "*You* may; and Rab, if he will behave himself." "I'se warrant he's do that, doctor;" and in slunk the faithful beast. I wish you could have seen him. There are no such dogs now. He belonged to a lost tribe. As I have said, he was brindled, and gray like Rubislaw granite; his hair short, hard, and close, like a lion's; his body thick-set, like a little bull—a sort of compressed Hercules of a dog. He must have been ninety pounds' weight, at the least; he had a large blunt head; his muzzle black as night, his mouth blacker than any night, a tooth or two—being all he had—gleaming out of his jaws of darkness. His head was scarred with the records of old wounds, a sort of series of fields of battle all over it; one eye out, one ear cropped as close as was Archbishop Leighton's father's; the remaining eye had the power of two; and above it, and in constant communication with it, was a tattered rag of an ear, which was forever unfurling itself, like an old flag; and then that bud of a tail, about one inch long, if it could in any sense be said to be long, being as broad as long—the mobility, the instantaneousness of that bud were very funny and surprising, and its expressive twinklings and winkings, the intercommunications between the eye, the ear, and it, were of the oddest and swiftest.

Rab had the dignity and simplicity of great size; and, having fought his way all along the road to absolute supremacy, he was as mighty in his own line as Julius Caesar or the Duke of Wellington, and had the gravity[3] of all great fighters.

You must have often observed the likeness of certain men to

certain animals, and of certain dogs to men. Now, I never looked at Rab without thinking of the great Baptist preacher, Andrew Fuller.[4] The same large, heavy, menacing, combative, sombre, honest countenance, the same deep inevitable eye, the same look—as of thunder asleep, but ready—neither a dog nor a man to be trifled with.

Next day, my master, the surgeon, examined Ailie. There was no doubt it must kill her, and soon. It could be removed; it might never return; it would give her speedy relief: she should have it done. She courtesied, looked at James, and said, "When?" "To-morrow," said the kind surgeon, a man of few words. She and James and Rab and I retired. I noticed that he and she spoke little, but seemed to anticipate everything in each other.

The following day, at noon, the students came in, hurrying up the great stair. At the first landing-place, on a small well-known black board, was a bit of paper fastened by wafers, and many remains of old wafers beside it. On the paper were the words, "An operation to-day.—*J.B., Clerk*"

Up ran the youths, eager to secure good places: in they crowded, full of interest and talk. "What's the case?" "Which side is it?"

Don't think them heartless; they are neither better nor worse than you or I; they get over their professional horrors, and into their proper work; and in them pity, as an *emotion*, ending in itself or at best in tears and a long-drawn breath, lessens, while pity, as a *motive*, is quickened, and gains power and purpose. It is well for poor human nature that it is so.

The operating theatre is crowded; much talk and fun, and all the cordiality and stir of youth. The surgeon with his staff of assistants is there. In comes Ailie: one look at her quiets and abates the eager students. That beautiful old woman is too much for them; they sit down, and are dumb, and gaze at her. These rough boys feel the power of her presence. She walks in quickly, but without haste; dressed in her mutch, her neckerchief, her white dimity short-gown, her black bombazine petticoat, showing her white worsted stockings and her carpet shoes. Behind her was James with Rab. James sat down in the distance, and took that huge and noble head between his knees. Rab looked perplexed and dangerous; forever cocking his ear and dropping it as fast.

Ailie stepped up on a seat, and laid herself on the table, as her friend the surgeon told her; arranged herself, gave a rapid look at James, shut her eyes, rested herself on me, and took my hand. The operation was at once begun; it was necessarily slow; and chloroform—one of God's best gifts to his suffering children—was then unknown. The surgeon did his work. The pale face showed its pain, but was still and silent. Rab's soul was working within him; he saw that something strange was going on, blood flowing from his mistress, and she suffering; his ragged ear was up, and importunate; he growled and gave now and then a sharp impatient yelp; he would have liked to have done something to that man. But James had him firm, and gave him a *glower* from time to time, and an intimation of a possible kick; all the better for James, it kept his eye and his mind off Ailie.

It is over: she is dressed, steps gently and decently down from the table, looks for James; then, turning to the surgeon and the students, she courtesies, and in a low, clear voice begs their pardon if she has behaved ill. The students—all of us—wept like children; the surgeon happed her up carefully, and, resting on James and me, Ailie went to her room, Rab following. We put her to bed. James took off his heavy shoes, crammed with tackets, heel-capt and toe-capt, and put them carefully under the table, saying, "Maister John, I'm for nane o' yer strynge nurse bodies for Ailie. I'll be her nurse, and I'll gang aboot on my stockin' soles as canny as pussy." And so he did; and handy and clever and swift and tender as any woman was that horny-handed, snell, peremptory little man. Everything she got he gave her: he seldom slept; and often I saw his small shrewd eyes out of the darkness, fixed on her. As before, they spoke little.

Rab behaved well, never moving, showing us how meek and gentle he could be, and occasionally, in his sleep, letting us know that he was demolishing some adversary. He took a walk with me every day, generally to the Candlemaker Row; but he was sombre and mild, declined doing battle, though some fit cases offered, and indeed submitted to sundry indignities, and was always very ready to turn, and came faster back, and trotted up the stair with much lightness, and went straight to that door. Jess, the mare, had been sent, with her weather-worn cart, to Howgate, and had doubtless her own dim and placid meditations and confusions on the absence of her master and Rab and her unnatural freedom from the road and her cart.

For some days Ailie did well. The wound healed "by the first intention;" for, as James said, "Oor Ailie's skin's ower clean to beil." The students came in quiet and anxious, and surrounded her bed. She said she liked to see their young, honest faces. The surgeon dressed her, and spoke to her in his own short kind way, pitying her through his eyes, Rab and James outside the circle,— Rab being now reconciled, and even cordial, and having made up his mind that as yet nobody required worrying, but, as you may suppose, semper paratus.

So far well; but four days after the operation my patient had a sudden and long shivering, a "groosin'," as she called it. I saw her soon after; her eyes were too bright, her cheek colored; she was restless, and ashamed of being so; the balance was lost; mischief had begun. On looking at the wound, a blush of red told the secret: her pulse was rapid, her breathing anxious and quick; she wasn't herself, as she said, and was vexed at her restlessness. We tried what we could. James did everything, was everywhere; never in the way, never out of it; Rab subsided under the table into a dark place, and was motionless, all but his eye, which followed every one. Ailie got worse; began to wander in her mind, gently; was more demonstrative in her ways to James, rapid in her questions, and sharp at times. He was vexed, and said, "She was never that way afore—no, never." For a time she knew her head was wrong, and was always asking our pardon, the dear, gentle old woman: then delirium set in strong, without pause. Her brain gave way, and then came that terrible spectacle,

"The intellectual power, through words and things,
Went sounding on its dim and perilous way;"

she sang bits of old songs and Psalms, stopping suddenly, mingling the Psalms of David, and the diviner words of his Son and Lord, with homely odds and ends and scraps of ballads.

Nothing more touching, or in a sense more strangely beautiful, did I ever witness. Her tremulous, rapid, affectionate, eager, Scotch voice, the swift, aimless, bewildered mind, the baffled utterance, the bright and perilous eye, some wild words, some household cares, something for James, the names of the dead, Rab called rapidly and in a "fremyt" voice, and he starting up, surprised, and slinking off as if he were to blame somehow, or had been dreaming he heard. Many eager questions and beseechings which James and I could make nothing of, and on which she seemed to set her all and then sink back ununderstood. It was very sad, but better than many things that are not called sad. James hovered about, put out and miserable, but active and exact as ever; read to her, when there was a lull, short bits from the Psalms, prose and metre, chanting the latter in his own rude and serious way, showing great knowledge of the fit words, bearing up like a man, and doting over her as his "ain Ailie." "Ailie, ma woman!" "Ma ain bonnie wee dawtie!"

The end was drawing on: the golden bowl was breaking; the silver cord was fast being loosed; that animula blandula, vagula, hospes, comesque, was about to flee. The body and the soul—companions for sixty years—were being sundered, and taking leave. She was walking, alone, through the valley of that shadow into which one day we must all enter; and yet she was not alone, for we know whose rod and staff were comforting her. One night she had fallen quiet, and, as we hoped, asleep; her eyes were shut. We put down the gas, and sat watching her. Suddenly she sat up in bed, and, taking a bed-gown which was lying on it rolled up, she held it eagerly to her breast, to the right side. We could see her eyes bright with a surprising tenderness and joy, bending over this bundle of clothes. She held it as a woman holds her sucking child; opening out her night-gown impatiently, and holding it close, and brooding over it, and murmuring foolish little words, as over one whom his mother comforteth, and who sucks and is satisfied. It was pitiful and strange to see her wasted dying look, keen and yet vague, her immense love.

"Preserve me!" groaned James, giving way. And then she rocked backward and forward, as if to make it sleep, hushing it, and wasting on it her infinite fondness. "Wae's me, doctor! I declare she's thinkin' it's that bairn." "What bairn?" "The only bairn we ever had; our wee Mysie, and she's in the Kingdom forty years and mair." It was plainly true: the pain in the breast, telling its urgent story to a bewildered, ruined brain, was misread and mistaken; it suggested to her the uneasiness of a breast full of milk, and then the child; and so again once more they were together, and she had her ain wee Mysie in her bosom.

This was the close. She sank rapidly: the delirium left her; but, as she whispered, she was "clean silly;" it was the lightening before the final darkness. After having for some time lain still, her eyes shut, she said, "James!" He came close to her, and, lifting up her calm, clear, beautiful eyes, she gave him a long look, turned to me kindly but shortly, looked for Rab but could not see him, then turned to her husband again, as if she would never leave off looking, shut her eyes and composed herself. She lay for some time breathing quick, and passed away so gently that, when we thought she was gone, James, in his old-fashioned way, held the mirror to her face. After a long pause, one small spot of dimness was breathed out; it vanished away, and never returned, leaving the blank clear darkness without a stain. "What is our life? it is even a vapor, which appeareth for a little time, and then vanisheth away."

Rab all this time had been fully awake and motionless: he came forward beside us: Ailie's hand, which James had held, was hanging down; it was soaked with his tears; Rab licked it all over carefully, looked at her, and returned to his place under the table.

James and I sat, I don't know how long, but for some time, saying nothing: he started up abruptly, and with some noise went to the table, and, putting his right fore and middle fingers each into a shoe, pulled them out, and put them on, breaking one of the leather latchets, and muttering in anger, "I never did the like o' that afore!"

I believe he never did; nor after either. "Rab!" he said, roughly, and pointing with his thumb to the bottom of the bed. Rab leaped up, and settled himself, his head and eye to the dead face. "Maister John, ye'll wait for me," said the carrier; and disappeared in the darkness, thundering downstairs in his heavy shoes. I ran to a front window; there he was, already round the house, and out at the gate, fleeing like a shadow.

I was afraid about him, and yet not afraid: so I sat down beside Rab, and, being wearied, fell asleep. I awoke from a sudden noise outside. It was November, and there had been a heavy fall of snow.

Rab was in statu quo; he heard the noise too, and plainly knew it, but never moved. I looked out; and there, at the gate, in the dim morning, for the sun was not up, was Jess and the cart, a cloud of steam rising from the old mare. I did not see James; he was already at the door, and came up the stairs and met me. It was less than three hours since he left, and he must have posted out—who knows how?—to Howgate, full nine miles off, yoked Jess, and driven her astonished into town. He had an armful of blankets, and was streaming with perspiration. He nodded to me, spread out on the floor two pairs of clean old blankets having at their corners "A. G., 1794," in large letters in red worsted. These were the initials of Alison Graeme, and James may have looked in at her from without—himself unseen but not unthought of—when he was "wat, wat, and weary," and, after having walked many a mile over the hills, may have seen her sitting, while "a' the lave were sleepin'," and by the firelight working her name on the blankets for her ain James's bed.

He motioned Rab down, and, taking his wife in his arms, laid her in the blankets, and happed her carefully and firmly up, leaving the face uncovered; and then, lifting her, he nodded again sharply to me, and, with a resolved but utterly miserable face, strode along the passage, and down-stairs, followed by Rab. I followed with a light; but he didn't need it. I went out, holding stupidly the candle in my hand in the calm frosty air; we were soon at the gate. I could have helped him, but I saw he was not to be meddled with, and he was strong and did not need it. He laid her down as tenderly, as safely, as he had lifted her out ten days before, as tenderly as when he had her first in his arms when she was only "A. G.," sorted her, leaving that beautiful sealed face open to the heavens; and then, taking Jess by the head, he moved away. He did not notice me; neither did Rab, who presided behind the cart.

I stood till they passed through the long shadow of the College and turned up Nicolson Street. I heard the solitary cart sound through the streets and die away and come again; and I returned, thinking of that company going up Libberton Brae, then along Roslin Muir, the morning light touching the Pentlands and making them like on-looking ghosts, then down the hill through Auchindinny woods, past "haunted Woodhouselee;" and as daybreak came sweeping up the bleak Lammermuirs, and fell on his own door, the company would stop, and James would take the key, and lift Ailie up again, laying her on her own bed, and, having put Jess up, would return with Rab and shut the door.

James buried his wife, with his neighbors mourning, Rab watching the proceedings from a distance. It was snow, and that black ragged hole would look strange in the midst of the swelling spotless cushion of white. James looked after everything; then rather suddenly fell ill, and took to bed; was insensible when the doctor came, and soon died. A sort of low fever was prevailing in the village, and his want of sleep, his exhaustion, and his misery made him apt to take it. The grave was not difficult to reopen. A fresh fall of snow had again made all things white and smooth; Rab once more looked on, and slunk home to the stable.

And what of Rab? I asked for him next week at the new carrier who got the good-will of James's business and was now master of Jess and her cart. "How's Rab?" He put me off, and said, rather rudely, "What's *your* business wi' the dowg?" I was not to be so put off. "Where's Rab?" He, getting confused and red, and intermeddling with his hair, said, "'Deed, sir, Rab's deid." "Dead! what did he die of?" "Weel, sir," said he, getting redder, "he didna exactly dee; he was killed. I had to brain him wi' a rackpin; there was nae doin' wi' him. He lay in the treviss wi' the mear, and wadna come oot. I tempit him wi' kail and meat, but he wad tak' naething, and keepit me fra feedin' the beast, and he was aye gur gurrin', and grup gruppin' me by the legs. I was laith to mak' awa wi' the auld dowg, his like wasna atween this and Thornhill,—but, 'deed, sir, I could do naething else." I believed him. Fit end for Rab, quick and complete. His teeth and his friends gone, why should he keep the peace and be civil?

He was buried in the braeface, near the burn, the children of the village, his companions, who used to make very free with him and sit on his ample stomach as he lay half asleep at the door in the sun, watching the solemnity.

Footnotes

1. It is not easy giving this look by one word: it was expressive of her being so much of her life alone.

2. "Black brows, they say, Become some women best; so that there be not Too much hair there, *but in a semicircle or a half-moon made with a pen.*" —*A Winter's Tale.*

3. A Highland game-keeper, when asked why a certain terrier, of singular pluck, was so much more solemn than the other dogs, said, "Oh, sir, life's full o' sairiousness to him: he just never can get eneuch o' fechtin'."

4. Fuller was in early life, when a farmer lad at Soham, famous as a boxer; not quarrelsome, but not without "the stern delight" a man of strength and courage feels in their exercise. Dr. Charles Stewart, of Dunearn, whose rare gifts and graces as a physician, a divine, a scholar, and a gentleman live only in the memory of those few who knew and survive him, liked to tell how Mr. Fuller used to say that when he was in the pulpit, and saw a buirdly man come along the passage, he would instinctively draw himself up, measure his imaginary antagonist, and

forecast how he would deal with him, his hands meanwhile condensing into fists and tending to "square." He must have been a hard hitter if he boxed as he preached,—what "The Fancy" would call an "ugly customer."

A Dog's Tale
Mark Twain

Chapter I

My father was a St. Bernard, my mother was a Collie, but I am a Presbyterian. This is what my mother told me, I do not know these nice distinctions myself. To me they are only fine large words meaning nothing. My mother had a fondness for such; she liked to say them, and see other dogs look surprised and envious, as wondering how she got so much education. But, indeed, it was not real education; it was only show: she got the words by listening in the dining-room and drawing-room when there was company, and by going with the children to Sunday-school and listening there; and whenever she heard a large word she said it over to herself many times, and so was able to keep it until there was a dogmatic gathering in the neighborhood, then she would get it off, and surprise and distress them all, from pocket-pup to mastiff, which rewarded her for all her trouble. If there was a stranger he was nearly sure to be suspicious, and when he got his breath again he would ask her what it meant. And she always told him. He was never expecting this but thought he would catch her; so when she told him, he was the one that looked ashamed, whereas he had thought it was going to be she. The others were always waiting for this, and glad of it and proud of her, for they knew what was going to happen, because they had had experience. When she told the meaning of a big word they were all so taken up with admiration that it never occurred to any dog to doubt if it was the right one; and that was natural, because, for one thing, she answered up so promptly that it seemed like a dictionary speaking, and for another thing, where could they find out whether it was right or not? for she was the only cultivated dog there was. By and by, when I was older, she brought home the word Unintellectual, one time, and worked it pretty hard all the week at different gatherings, making much unhappiness and despondency; and it was at this time that I noticed that during that week she was asked for the meaning at eight different assemblages, and flashed out a fresh definition every time, which showed me that she had more presence of mind than culture, though I said nothing, of course. She had one word which she always kept on hand, and ready, like a life-preserver, a kind of emergency word to strap on when she was likely to get washed overboard in a sudden way—that was the word Synonymous. When she happened to fetch out a long word which had had its day weeks before and its prepared meanings gone to her dump-pile, if there was a stranger there of course it knocked him groggy for a couple of minutes, then he would come to, and by that time she would be away down wind on another tack, and not expecting anything; so when he'd hail and ask her to cash in, I (the only dog on the inside of her game) could see her canvas flicker a moment—but only just a moment—then it would belly out taut and full, and she would say, as calm as a summer's day, "It's synonymous with supererogation," or some godless long reptile of a word like that, and go placidly about and skim away on the next tack, perfectly comfortable, you know, and leave that stranger looking profane and embarrassed, and the initiated slatting the floor with their tails in unison and their faces transfigured with a holy joy.

And it was the same with phrases. She would drag home a whole phrase, if it had a grand sound, and play it six nights and two matinees, and explain it a new way every time—which she had to, for all she cared for was the phrase; she wasn't interested in what it meant, and knew those dogs hadn't wit enough to catch her, anyway. Yes, she was a daisy! She got so she wasn't afraid of anything, she had such confidence in the ignorance of those creatures. She even brought anecdotes that she had heard the family and the dinner-guests laugh and shout over; and as a rule she got the nub of one chestnut hitched onto another chestnut, where, of course, it didn't fit and hadn't any point; and when she delivered the nub she fell over and rolled on the floor and laughed and barked in the most insane way, while I could see that she was wondering to herself why it didn't seem as funny as it did when she first heard it. But no harm was done; the others rolled and barked too, privately ashamed of themselves for not seeing the point, and never suspecting that the fault was not with them and there wasn't any to see.

You can see by these things that she was of a rather vain and frivolous character; still, she had virtues, and enough to make up, I think. She had a kind heart and gentle ways, and never harbored resentments for injuries done her, but put them easily out of her mind and forgot them; and she taught her children her kindly way, and from her we learned also to be brave and prompt in time of danger, and not to run away, but face the peril that threatened friend or stranger, and help him the best we could without stopping to think what the cost might be to us. And she taught us not by words only, but by example, and that is the best way and the surest and the most lasting. Why, the brave things she did, the splendid things! she was just a soldier; and so modest about it—well, you couldn't help admiring her, and you couldn't help imitating her; not even a King Charles spaniel could remain entirely despicable in her society. So, as you see, there was more to her than her education.

Chapter II

When I was well grown, at last, I was sold and taken away, and I never saw her again. She was broken-hearted, and so was I, and we cried; but she comforted me as well as she could, and said we were sent into this world for a wise and good purpose, and must do our duties without repining, take our life as we might find it, live it for the best good of others, and never mind about the results; they were not our affair. She said men who did like this would have a noble and beautiful reward by and by in another world, and although we animals would not go there, to do well and right without reward would give to our brief lives a worthiness and dignity which in itself would be a reward. She had gathered these things from time to time when she had gone to the Sunday-school with the children, and had laid them up in her memory more carefully than she had done with those other words and phrases; and she had studied them deeply, for her good and ours. One may see by this that she had a wise and thoughtful head, for all there was so much lightness and vanity in it.

So we said our farewells, and looked our last upon each other through our tears; and the last thing she said—keeping it for the last to make me remember it the better, I think—was, "In memory of me, when there is a time of danger to another do not think of yourself, think of your mother, and do as she would do."

Do you think I could forget that? No.

A Dog's Tale

Chapter III

It was such a charming home!—my new one; a fine great house, with pictures, and delicate decorations, and rich furniture, and no gloom anywhere, but all the wilderness of dainty colors lit up with flooding sunshine; and the spacious grounds around it, and the great garden—oh, greensward, and noble trees, and flowers, no end! And I was the same as a member of the family; and they loved me, and petted me, and did not give me a new name, but called me by my old one that was dear to me because my mother had given it me—Aileen Mavourneen. She got it out of a song; and the Grays knew that song, and said it was a beautiful name.

Mrs. Gray was thirty, and so sweet and so lovely, you cannot imagine it; and Sadie was ten, and just like her mother, just a darling slender little copy of her, with auburn tails down her back, and short frocks; and the baby was a year old, and plump and dimpled, and fond of me, and never could get enough of hauling on my tail, and hugging me, and laughing out its innocent happiness; and Mr. Gray was thirty-eight, and tall and slender and handsome, a little bald in front, alert, quick in his movements, business-like, prompt, decided, unsentimental, and with that kind of trim-chiseled face that just seems to glint and sparkle with frosty intellectuality! He was a renowned scientist. I do not know what the word means, but my mother would know how to use it and get effects. She would know how to depress a rat-terrier with it and make a lap-dog look sorry he came. But that is not the best one; the best one was Laboratory. My mother could organize a Trust on that one that would skin the tax-collars off the whole herd. The laboratory was not a book, or a picture, or a place to wash your hands in, as the college president's dog said—no, that is the lavatory; the laboratory is quite different, and is filled with jars, and bottles, and electrics, and wires, and strange machines; and every week other scientists came there and sat in the place, and used the machines, and discussed, and made what they called experiments and discoveries; and often I came, too, and stood around and listened, and tried to learn, for the sake of my mother, and in loving memory of her, although it was a pain to me, as realizing what she was losing out of her life and I gaining nothing at all; for try as I might, I was never able to make anything out of it at all.

Other times I lay on the floor in the mistress's work-room and slept, she gently using me for a foot-stool, knowing it pleased me, for it was a caress; other times I spent an hour in the nursery, and got well tousled and made happy; other times I watched by the crib there, when the baby was asleep and the nurse out for a few minutes on the baby's affairs; other times I romped and raced through the grounds and the garden with Sadie till we were tired out, then slumbered on the grass in the shade of a tree while she read her book; other times I went visiting among the neighbor dogs—for there were some most pleasant ones not far away, and one very handsome and courteous and graceful one, a curly-haired Irish setter by the name of Robin Adair, who was a Presbyterian like me, and belonged to the Scotch minister.

The servants in our house were all kind to me and were fond of me, and so, as you see, mine was a pleasant life. There could not be a happier dog that I was, nor a gratefuller one. I will say this for myself, for it is only the truth: I tried in all ways to do well and right, and honor my mother's memory and her teachings, and earn the happiness that had come to me, as best I could.

By and by came my little puppy, and then my cup was full, my happiness was perfect. It was the dearest little waddling thing, and so smooth and soft and velvety, and had such cunning little awkward paws, and such affectionate eyes, and such a sweet and innocent face; and it made me so proud to see how the children and their mother adored it, and fondled it, and exclaimed over every little wonderful thing it did. It did seem to me that life was just too lovely to—

Then came the winter. One day I was standing a watch in the nursery. That is to say, I was asleep on the bed. The baby was asleep in the crib, which was alongside the bed, on the side next the fireplace. It was the kind of crib that has a lofty tent over it made of gauzy stuff that you can see through. The nurse was out, and we two sleepers were alone. A spark from the wood-fire was shot out, and it lit on the slope of the tent. I suppose a quiet interval followed, then a scream from the baby awoke me, and there was that tent flaming up toward the ceiling! Before I could think, I sprang to the floor in my fright, and in a second was half-way to the door; but in the next half-second my mother's farewell was sounding in my ears, and I was back on the bed again. I reached my head through the flames and dragged the baby out by the waist-band, and tugged it along, and we fell to the floor together in a cloud of smoke; I snatched a new hold, and dragged the screaming little creature along and out at the door and around the bend of the hall, and was still tugging away, all excited and happy and proud, when the master's voice shouted:

"Begone you cursed beast!" and I jumped to save myself; but he was furiously quick, and chased me up, striking furiously at me with his cane, I dodging this way and that, in terror, and at last a strong blow fell upon my left foreleg, which made me shriek and fall, for the moment, helpless; the cane went up for another blow, but never descended, for the nurse's voice rang wildly out, "The nursery's on fire!" and the master rushed away in that direction, and my other bones were saved.

The pain was cruel, but, no matter, I must not lose any time; he might come back at any moment; so I limped on three legs to the other end of the hall, where there was a dark little stairway leading up into a garret where old boxes and such things were kept, as I had heard say, and where people seldom went. I managed to climb up there, then I searched my way through the dark among the piles of things, and hid in the secretest place I could find. It was foolish to be afraid there, yet still I was; so afraid that I held in and hardly even whimpered, though it would have been such a comfort to whimper, because that eases the pain, you know. But I could lick my leg, and that did some good.

For half an hour there was a commotion downstairs, and shoutings, and rushing footsteps, and then there was quiet again. Quiet for some minutes, and that was grateful to my spirit, for then my fears began to go down; and fears are worse than pains—oh, much worse. Then came a sound that froze me. They were calling me—calling me by name—hunting for me!

It was muffled by distance, but that could not take the terror out of it, and it was the most dreadful sound to me that I had ever heard. It went all about, everywhere, down there: along the halls, through all the rooms, in both stories, and in the basement and the cellar; then outside, and farther and farther away—then back, and all about the house again, and I thought it would never, never stop. But at last it did, hours and hours after the vague twilight of the garret had long ago been blotted out by black darkness.

Then in that blessed stillness my terrors fell little by little away, and I was at peace and slept. It was a good rest I had, but I woke before the twilight had come again. I was feeling fairly comfortable, and I could think out a plan now. I made a very good one; which was, to creep down, all the way down the back stairs, and hide behind the cellar door, and slip out and escape when the iceman came at dawn, while he was inside filling the refrigerator; then I would hide all day, and start on my journey when night came; my journey to—well, anywhere where they would not know me and betray me to the master. I was feeling almost cheerful now; then suddenly I thought: Why, what would life be without my puppy!

That was despair. There was no plan for me; I saw that; I must stay where I was; stay, and wait, and take what might come—it was not my affair; that was what life is—my mother had said it. Then— well, then the calling began again! All my sorrows came back. I said to myself, the master will never forgive. I did not know what I had done to make him so bitter and so unforgiving, yet I judged it was something a dog could not understand, but which was clear to a man and dreadful.

They called and called—days and nights, it seemed to me. So long that the hunger and thirst near drove me mad, and I recognized that I was getting very weak. When you are this way you sleep a great deal, and I did. Once I woke in an awful fright—it seemed to me that the calling was right there in the garret! And so it was: it was Sadie's voice, and she was crying; my name was falling from her lips all broken, poor thing, and I could not believe my ears for the joy of it when I heard her say:

"Come back to us—oh, come back to us, and forgive—it is all so sad without our—"

I broke in with *such* a grateful little yelp, and the next moment Sadie was plunging and stumbling through the darkness and the lumber and shouting for the family to hear, "She's found, she's found!"

The days that followed—well, they were wonderful. The mother and Sadie and the servants—why, they just seemed to worship me. They couldn't seem to make me a bed that was fine enough; and as for food, they couldn't be satisfied with anything but game and delicacies that were out of season; and every day the friends and neighbors flocked in to hear about my heroism—that was the name they called it by, and it means agriculture. I remember my mother pulling it on a kennel once, and explaining it in that way, but didn't say what agriculture was, except that it was synonymous with intramural incandescence; and a dozen times a day Mrs. Gray and Sadie would tell the tale to new-comers, and say I risked my life to say the baby's, and both of us had burns to prove it, and then the company would pass me around and pet me and exclaim about me, and you could see the pride in the eyes of Sadie and her mother; and when the people wanted to know what made me limp, they looked ashamed and changed the subject, and sometimes when people hunted them this way and that way with questions about it, it looked to me as if they were going to cry.

And this was not all the glory; no, the master's friends came, a whole twenty of the most distinguished people, and had me in the laboratory, and discussed me as if I was a kind of discovery; and some of them said it was wonderful in a dumb beast, the finest exhibition of instinct they could call to mind; but the master said, with vehemence, "It's far above instinct; it's *reason*, and many a man, privileged to be saved and go with you and me to a better world by right of its possession, has less of it that this poor silly quadruped that's foreordained to perish;" and then he laughed, and said: "Why, look at me—I'm a sarcasm! bless you, with all my grand intelligence, the only thing I inferred was that the dog had gone mad and was destroying the child, whereas but for the beast's intelligence—it's *reason*, I tell you!—the child would have perished!"

They disputed and disputed, and I was the very center of subject of it all, and I wished my mother could know that this grand honor had come to me; it would have made her proud.

Then they discussed optics, as they called it, and whether a certain injury to the brain would produce blindness or not, but they could not agree about it, and said they must test it by experiment by and by; and next they discussed plants, and that interested me, because in the summer Sadie and I had planted seeds—I helped her dig the holes, you know—and after days and days a little shrub or a flower came up there, and it was a wonder how that could happen; but it did, and I wished I could talk—I would have told those people about it and shown then how much I knew, and been all alive with the subject; but I didn't care for the optics; it was dull, and when they came back to it again it bored me, and I went to sleep.

Pretty soon it was spring, and sunny and pleasant and lovely, and the sweet mother and the children patted me and the puppy good-by, and went away on a journey and a visit to their kin, and the master wasn't any company for us, but we played together and had good times, and the servants were kind and friendly, so we got along quite happily and counted the days and waited for the family.

And one day those men came again, and said, now for the test, and they took the puppy to the laboratory, and I limped three-leggedly along, too, feeling proud, for any attention shown to the puppy was a pleasure to me, of course. They discussed and experimented, and then suddenly the puppy shrieked, and they set him on the floor, and he went staggering around, with his head all bloody, and the master clapped his hands and shouted:

"There, I've won—confess it! He's as blind as a bat!"

And they all said:"It's so—you've proved your theory, and suffering humanity owes you a great debt from henceforth," and they crowded around him, and wrung his hand cordially and thankfully, and praised him.

But I hardly saw or heard these things, for I ran at once to my little darling, and snuggled close to it where it lay, and licked the blood, and it put its head against mine, whimpering softly, and I knew in my heart it was a comfort to it in its pain and trouble to feel its mother's touch, though it could not see me. Then it dropped down, presently, and its little velvet nose rested upon the floor, and it was still, and did not move any more.

Soon the master stopped discussing a moment, and rang in the footman, and said, "Bury it in the far corner of the garden," and then went on with the discussion, and I trotted after the footman, very happy and grateful, for I knew the puppy was out of its pain now, because it was asleep. We went far down the garden to the farthest end, where the children and the nurse and the puppy and I used to play in the summer in the shade of a great elm, and there the footman dug a hole, and I saw he was going to plant the puppy, and I was glad, because it would grow and come up a fine handsome dog, like Robin Adair, and be a beautiful surprise for the family when they came home; so I tried to help him dig, but my lame leg was no good, being stiff, you know, and you have to have two, or it is nouse. When the footman had finished and covered little Robin up, he patted my head, and there were tears in his eyes, and he said: "Poor little doggie, you saved *his* child!"

I have watched two whole weeks, and he doesn't come up! This last week a fright has been stealing upon me. I think there is something terrible about this. I do not know what it is, but the fear makes me sick, and I cannot eat, though the servants bring me the best of food; and they pet me so, and even come in the night, and cry, and say, "Poor doggie—do give it up and come home; don't break our hearts!" and all this terrifies me the more, and makes me sure something has happened. And I am so weak; since yesterday I cannot stand on my feet anymore. And within this hour the servants, looking toward the sun where it was sinking out of sight and the night chill coming on, said things I could not understand, but they carried something cold to my heart.

"Those poor creatures! They do not suspect. They will come home in the morning, and eagerly ask for the little doggie that did the brave deed, and who of us will be strong enough to say the truth to them: 'The humble little friend is gone where go the beasts that perish.'"

A Brave Dog
Sir Samuel W. Baker

When I was a boy, my grandfather frequently told a story concerning a dog which he knew, as a more than ordinary example of the fidelity so frequently exhibited by the race. This animal was a mastiff that belonged to an intimate friend, to whom it was a constant companion. It was an enormous specimen of that well-known breed, which is not generally celebrated for any peculiar intelligence, but is chiefly remarkable for size and strength. This dog had been brought up by its master from puppyhood, and as the proprietor was a single man, there had been no division of affection, as there would have been had the dog belonged to a family of several members. Turk regarded nobody but his owner. (I shall now honour Turk by the masculine gender.)

Whenever Mr. Prideaux went out for a walk, Turk was sure to be near his heels. Street dogs would bark and snarl at the giant as his massive form attracted their attention, but Turk seldom condescended to notice such vulgar demonstrations; he was a noble-looking creature, somewhat resembling a small lioness; but although he was gentle and quiet in disposition, he had upon several occasions been provoked beyond endurance, and his attack had been nearly always fatal to his assailants. He slept at night outside his master's door, and no sentry could be more alert upon his watch than the faithful dog, who had apparently only one ambition—to protect, and to accompany his owner.

Mr. Prideaux had a dinner-party. He never invited ladies, but simply entertained his friends as a bachelor; his dinners were but secondary to the quality of his guests, however, who were always men of reputation either in the literary world, or in the modern annals of society. The dog Turk was invariably present, and usually stretched his huge form upon the hearth-rug.

It was a cold night in winter, when Mr. Prideaux's friends were talking after dinner, that the conversation turned upon the subject of dogs. Almost every person had an anecdote to relate, and my own grandfather being present, had no doubt added his mite to the collection, when Turk suddenly awoke from a sound sleep, and having stretched himself until he appeared to be awake to the situation, walked up to his master's side, and rested his large head upon the table.

"Ha ha, Turk!" exclaimed Mr. Prideaux, "you must have heard our arguments about the dogs, so you have put in an appearance."

"And a magnificent specimen he is!" remarked my grandfather; "but although a mastiff is the largest and most imposing of the race, I do not think it is as sensible as many others."

"As a rule you are right," replied his master, "because they are generally chained up as watch-dogs, and have not the intimate association with human beings which is so great an advantage to house-dogs; but Turk has been my constant companion from the first month of his existence, and his intelligence is very remarkable. He understands most things that I say, if they are connected with himself; he will often lie upon the rug with his large eyes fixed upon me as though searching my inward thoughts, and he will frequently be aware instinctively that I wish to go out; upon such times he will fetch my hat, cane, or gloves, whichever may be at hand, and wait for me at the front door. He will take a letter or any other token to several houses of my acquaintance, and wait for a reply; and he can perform a variety of actions that would imply a share of reason seldom possessed by other dogs."

A smile of incredulity upon several faces was at once perceived by Mr. Prideaux, who immediately took a guinea from his pocket, and addressed his dog. "Here, Turk! they won't believe in you!...take this guinea to No.--,--Street, to Mr.--, and bring me a receipt."

The dog wagged his huge tail with evident pleasure, and the guinea having been placed in his mouth, he hastened towards the door; this being opened, he was admitted through the front entrance to the street. It was a miserable night; the wind was blowing the sleet and rain against the windows; the gutters were running with muddy water, and the weather was exactly that which is expressed by the common term, "not fit to turn a dog out in;" nevertheless, Turk had started upon his mission in the howling gale and darkness, while the front door was once more closed against the blast.

The party were comfortably seated around the fire, and much interested in the success or failure of the dog's adventure.

"How long will it be before we may expect Turk's return?" inquired an incredulous guest.

"The house to which I have sent him is about a mile and a half distant, therefore if there is no delay when he barks for admission at the door, and my friend is not absent from home, he should return in about three-quarters of an hour with an acknowledgment. If, on the other hand, he cannot gain admission, he may wait for any length of time," replied his master.

Bets were exchanged among the company—some supported the dog's chances of success, while others were against him.

The evening wore away; the allotted time was exceeded, and a whole hour had passed, but no dog had returned. Fresh bets were made, but the odds were against the dog. His master was still hopeful…. "I must tell you," said Mr. Prideaux, "that Turk frequently carries notes for me, and as he knows the house well, he certainly will not make a mistake; perhaps my friend may be dining out, in which case Turk will probably wait for a longer time"….Two hours passed…the storm was raging. Mr. Prideaux himself went to the front door, which flew open before a fierce gust the instant that the lock was turned. The clouds were rushing past a moon but faintly visible at short intervals, and the gutters were clogged with masses of half-melted snow. "Poor Turk!" muttered his master, "this is indeed a wretched night for you…. Perhaps they have kept you in the warm kitchen, and will not allow you to return in such fearful weather."

When Mr. Prideaux returned to his guests he could not conceal his disappointment. "Ha!" exclaimed one who had betted against the dog, "I never doubted his sagacity. With a guinea in his mouth, he has probably gone into some house of entertainment where dogs are supplied with dinner and a warm bed, instead of shivering in a winter's gale!"

Jokes were made by the winners of bets at the absent dog's expense, but his master was anxious and annoyed. The various bets were paid by the losers, and poor Turk's reputation had suffered severely…. It was long past midnight: the guests were departed, the storm was raging, and violent gusts occasionally shook the house…. Mr. Prideaux was alone in his study, and he poked the fire until it blazed and roared up the chimney….

"What can have become of that dog?" exclaimed his master to

himself, now really anxious; "I hope they kept him; …most likely they would not send him back upon such a dreadful night."

Mr. Prideaux's study was close to the front door, and his acute attention was suddenly directed to a violent shaking and scratching, accompanied by a prolonged whine. In an instant he ran into the hall, and unlocked the entrance door…. A mass of filth and mud entered…. This was Turk!

The dog seemed dreadfully fatigued, and was shivering with wet and cold. His usually clean coat was thick with mire, as though he had been dragged through deep mud. He wagged his tail when he heard his master's voice, but appeared dejected and ill.

Mr. Prideaux had rung the bell, and the servants, who were equally interested as their master in Turk's failure to perform his mission, had attended the summons. The dog was taken downstairs, and immediately placed in a large tub of hot water, in which he was accustomed to be bathed. It was now discovered that in addition to mud and dirt, which almost concealed his coat, he was besmeared with blood!

Mr. Prideaux himself sponged his favourite with hot soap and water, and, to his astonishment, he perceived wounds of a serious nature: the dog's throat was badly torn, his back and breast were deeply bitten, and there could be no doubt that he had been worried by a pack of dogs. This was a strange occurrence, that Turk should be discomfited!

He was now washed clean, and was being rubbed dry with a thick towel while he stood upon a blanket before the kitchen fire…. "Why, Turk, old boy, what has been the matter? Tell us all about it, poor old man!" exclaimed his master.

The dog was now thoroughly warmed, and he panted with the heat of the kitchen fire; he opened his mouth,…*and the guinea which he had received in trust dropped on the kitchen floor*!

"There is some mystery in this," said Mr. Prideaux, "which I will endeavour to discover to-morrow…. He has been set upon by strange dogs, and rather than lose the guinea, he has allowed himself to be half killed without once opening his mouth in self-defence! Poor Turk!" continued his master, "you must have lost your way, old man, in the darkness and storm; most likely confused after the unequal fight. What an example you have given us wretched humans in being steadfast to a trust!"

Turk was wonderfully better after his warm bath. He lapped up a large bowl of good thick soup mixed with bread, and in half an hour was comfortably asleep upon his thick rug by his master's bedroom door….

Upon the following morning the storm had cleared away, and a bright sky had succeeded to the gloom of the preceding night.

Immediately after breakfast, Mr. Prideaux, accompanied by his dog (who was, although rather stiff, not much the worse for the rough treatment he had received), started for a walk towards the house to which he had directed Turk upon the previous evening. He was anxious to discover whether his friend had been absent, as he concluded that the dog might have been waiting for admittance, and had been perhaps attacked by some dogs belonging to the house, or its neighbours'.

The master and Turk had walked for nearly a mile, and had just turned the corner of a street when, as they passed a butcher's shop upon the right hand, a large brindled mastiff rushed from the shop-door, and flew at Turk with unprovoked ferocity.

"Call your dog off!" shouted Mr. Prideaux to the butcher, who surveyed the attack with impudent satisfaction…. "Call him off, or my dog will kill him!" continued Mr. Prideaux.

The usually docile Turk had rushed to meet his assailant with a fury that was extraordinary. With a growl like that of a lion, he quickly seized his antagonist by the throat; rearing upon his hind legs, he exerted his tremendous strength, and in a fierce struggle of only a few seconds, he threw the brindled dog upon its back. It was in vain that Mr. Prideaux endeavoured to call him off, the rage of his favourite was quite ungovernable; he never for an instant relaxed his hold, but with the strength of a wild beast of prey, Turk shook the head of the butcher's dog to the right and left until it struck each time heavily against the pavement…. The butcher attempted to interfere, and lashed him with a huge whip.

"Stand clear! fair play! don't you strike my dog!" shouted Mr. Prideaux. "Your dog was the first to attack!"

In reply to the whip, Turk had redoubled his fury, and, without relinquishing his hold, he had now dragged the butcher's dog off the pavement, and occasionally shaking the body as he pulled the unresisting mass along the gutter, he drew it into the middle of the street.

A large crowd had collected, which completely stopped the thoroughfare. There were no police in those days, but only watchmen, who were few and far between; even had they been present, it is probable they would have joined in the amusement of a dog-fight, which in that age of brutality was considered to be sport….

"Fair play!" shouted the bystanders…. "Let 'em have it out!" cried others, as they formed a circle around the dogs…. In the meantime, Mr. Prideaux had seized Turk by his collar, while the butcher was endeavouring to release the remains of his dog from the infuriated and deadly grip….

At length Mr. Prideaux's voice and action appeared for a moment to create a calm, and, snatching the opportunity, he, with the assistance of a person in the crowd, held back his dog, as the carcass of the butcher's dog was dragged away by the lately insolent owner…. The dog was dead!

Turk's flanks were heaving with the intense exertion and excitement of the fight, and he strained to escape from his master's hold to once more attack the lifeless body of his late antagonist.... At length, by kind words and the caress of the well-known hand, his fury was calmed down....

"Well, that's the most curious adventure I've ever had with a dog!" exclaimed the butcher, who was now completely crestfallen.... "Why, that's the very dog! he is so—that's the very dog who came by my shop late last night in the howling storm, and my dog Tiger went at him and towzled him up completely. I never saw such a cowardly cur; he wouldn't show any fight, although he was pretty near as big as a costermonger's donkey; and there my dog Tiger nearly eat half of him, and dragged the other half about the gutter, till he looked more like an old door-mat than a dog; and I thought he must have killed him ... and here he comes out as fresh as paint to-day, and kills old Tiger clean off as though he'd been only a biggish cat!"

"What do you say?" asked Mr. Prideaux..."Was it your dog that worried my poor dog last night, when he was upon a message of trust?...My friend, I thank you for this communication, but let me inform you of the fact that my dog had *a guinea in his mouth* to carry to my friend, and rather than drop it he allowed himself to be half killed by your savage Tiger. To-day he has proved his courage, and your dog has discovered his mistake. This is the guinea that he dropped from his mouth when he returned to me after midnight, beaten and distressed!" said Mr. Prideaux, much excited. "Here, Turk, old boy, take the guinea again, and come along with me! you have had your revenge, and have given us all a lesson." His master gave him the guinea in his mouth, and they continued their walk.... It appeared, upon Mr. Prideaux's arrival at his friend's house, that

Turk had never been there; probably after his defeat he had become so confused that he lost his way in the heavy storm, and had at length regained the road home some time after midnight, in the deplorable condition already described.

Firehouse Annie
Karyn Kay Zweifel

The dog was stretched out full-length in the sun. An observer, looking close, could see little tendrils of steam rising from her well-muscled flanks. After a long, cold winter, Annie was making the most of the early spring sunshine pouring through the tall windows lining the south dormitory wall. She was alone upstairs—all six firefighters on duty were downstairs. There were a thousand small tasks to keep them occupied during daylight hours: the stable where Nell and Bramble lived was kept immaculate, the horses themselves needed grooming, and their halters and traces needed regular inspections for signs of wear, the firetruck always had a bolt to tighten or a wheel to adjust, and the hoses and pumps required checking.

Annie yawned and stretched. She reveled in the on-again, off-again urgency of her work. There was nothing like the excitement of a good run through the streets, some of them bricked—but most of them good old-fashioned dirt or mud, barking with all her might to accompany the wild clanging of the bell on the wagon. Nell and Bramble loved it, too. The three of them would race flat out to the scene of the fire, while passersby gaped and other traffic scurried out of the way. No one could deny the absolute necessity of their work; no one could resist admiring the spirit and grace with which they performed it.

The dog rose to her feet and padded across the room. Soon it would be time for supper, barring any calls, so now would be the best time to go pay a call on Nell and Bramble. The stable cat might be around, too, and that was always good for a little fun. Annie and the old tom had an agreement: He would allow himself to be chased about a third of the way down the block before he turned to make a stand. Annie would pretend to be vanquished, and both creatures would return to the firehouse. Annie enjoyed the excitement, and the tom appreciated the boost to his reputation as a tough old warrior.

Just as she began to descend the stairs, a wave of noise and activity broke over the station house. A clangorous bell ripped through the everyday hum of chores and conversation, and the firefighters began to run in every direction. To an untrained eye, it became bedlam. But Annie could see a precise, well-rehearsed pattern to the movement of the men. Tom and Harold literally jumped into their tall black boots and then snatched up their coats and shrugged them on as they ran across the yard to the stable. Red coiled the big canvas hose back into its place on the tank wagon, and Bobby tightened the bolts on the two front wheels. The Chief and Slim, the driver, conferred hastily over a map as they fastened their coats. Nell and Bramble were brought around and harnessed in a flash, and the wagon thundered out onto the street in less than three minutes after the alarm was rung, Annie running fleet by its side, and Red flailing the bell on the wagon with gusto.

They saw the smoke first, an angry black column rising rapidly up to the sky. It didn't waver on its course; that was good—there was no wind to aggravate the fire. When they reached the block of the fire, a crowd of onlookers scattered as Annie burst through ahead of the wagon, barking furiously.

It quickly became apparent that the fire was in an outbuilding behind the main building, but there was no easy access from the street. Annie tore around the corner, and Nell and Bramble followed close behind, the wagon careening after them. Nell and Bramble just barely caught sight of Annie's jaunty tail, a whip-like cord with a stylish black tip, as she darted into an alley. They followed and pulled up with a jerk right beside a little shed that was burning merrily. Nell, Bramble, and Annie had done their job—now the firefighters got to work.

This was the course of Annie's life—long, lazy stretches of inactivity broken by spurts of thrilling and dangerous activity, racing through the streets of her small city. People all over knew her by name.

"Here comes Annie," the owner of the diner might say, seeing a blur of sleek black and white sprinting by.

"Did you hear what happened last week? When the Morris's place caught on fire?" Someone was always on hand to tell a story about Annie. "I heard that the youngest, Mary, I think, had been carried out of the house lickety-split by her mama. But she was standing on the sidewalk crying like the world was ending."

The diner owner stopped polishing the counter and leaned over, his attention caught. "Annie was watching her—you know how she likes children—and darned if she didn't look like she was listening to that little girl. Then, before anyone could stop her, that crazy dog dashes up to the porch, flames shooting out of the windows and doors like that house was hell itself, snatches up something in her mouth, and comes bounding up to little Mary to lay it at her feet."

"What was it?"

"The little girl's doll—soaked and covered in soot, but safe. It was the most amazing thing. Mary's mama says she'll do anything for that dog. Says Annie's the closest thing to an angel that ever walked on four feet."

The owner of the diner shook his head, smiling, and the story was added to the growing collection of tales about amazing Annie.

One late fall day, a call came from the candy store downtown, on First Street near the river. When the firefighters arrived, the first floor of the brick building was already consumed by flames. The second and third floors were threatened, so the firefighters had their hands full. Unnoticed by them, Annie ran around to the back of the building where the owner had constructed a little lean-to for extra storage.

Bobby was directing a stream of water into the front window when Annie bounded up to him and began barking furiously. "What, Annie? I'm busy now!"

Annie wouldn't stop barking. "Red," the firefighter shouted, "come see what's wrong with Annie!"

The second firefighter shook his head when he saw the nar-row corridor between buildings that Annie intended him to pass through. "It's too dangerous, Annie," he said. "Come on—let's get back to work."

Then the dog did something so out of character that the firefighter was shocked. She ran behind him and turned to plant her feet, blocking his access back to the street—and she growled at him.

"This is really stupid, Annie," the firefighter protested, but he let her lead him through the passageway anyway.

Smoke was pouring out of the little lean-to. Red was horrified to see Annie run inside and then, almost immediately, begin to back out, obviously tugging hard on something many times her own weight. In spite of the heat and the showers of burning embers floating down from the main building, Red ran up to the little structure.

Annie was pulling hard on the belt of Mr. Patillo, the candy store owner—he'd been overcome by the smoke. Red grabbed the man and carried him to safety, Annie barking loudly at his heels.

Annie served the central fire station for eleven years before she died quietly in her sleep. Almost everyone in town had a story about a miraculous Annie rescue or a remarkable Annie feat. Her courage was legendary. The firefighters led a funeral procession through the streets, and she was buried in a corner of the yard next to the stables.

It wasn't even two years later that old Mr. Patillo reported seeing her again. "I swear to you by all that's holy, I saw that dog racing down the street!"

Mr. Patillo's son-in-law now ran the candy store, but he allowed the old man to sit around and tell his tall tales to the children who came in after school. "Papa, she died last year," he argued patiently. "They don't even have dogs anymore because they can't keep up with the new fire engine. You're seeing things in the rain."

Just then lightning flashed outside, and the rain poured down with renewed intensity. "I tell you, I saw her," the old man insisted stubbornly. "I think she was warning me."

"Warning you about what, Papa?" His son-in-law spoke kindly, but his tone was laced with a pity the old man despised.

"I don't know—a fire, maybe, or something. This rain. How high is the river?"

"They say it's going to stop raining tonight, and the river won't crest above flood level. Don't worry about it, Papa." The old man crossed his arms and sat like a stone on his stool behind the counter.

"Okay, then, worry about it—I don't care. I'll let you lock up. I'm taking the books home to work on them tonight. I'll see you in the morning." Mr. Patillo's son-in-law pulled the door shut. The little bell meant to announce customers jangled angrily.

The old man toiled for hours, watching through the big display window as the rain came down steadily. Up and down the stairs he walked carrying box after box of merchandise to an unused room on the second floor. Once, long after dark, he took his umbrella and went to stand at the edge of First Street. The river was lapping hungrily at the land, already out of bounds.

When he was finished, he climbed the stairs one last time to his apartment, empty now of his wife and his five noisy children. The sound of a bell woke him—it was the telephone, a contraption his daughter had insisted he install.

"What do you want?" he growled into the receiver. He didn't like the intrusion the little black instrument created.

"Papa, we're ruined!" It was his son-in-law. Mr. Patillo felt a small warm sense of satisfaction begin glowing in his stomach, which rapidly spread throughout his body.

"Have you looked out your window, Papa?"

Without a word, Mr. Patillo set the telephone down and crossed to the window. The sun had come out as promised. It sparkled and gleamed on the silvery surface of the water directly below him. The river had flooded in the night, and the store below was filled with five feet of river water.

"I've taken care of it, boy," he said gruffly to his son-in-law. "I moved the inventory upstairs last night."

In 1922, when Mr. Patillo's son-in-law was a cranky old man, he still told that story to anybody who'd listen. But Angie Lorino had no time to stop for an old man's tales. Her new husband ran a dry goods store on Third Street, and she had her hands full keeping it swept and stocked and waiting on the customers who were always in a hurry.

One afternoon in late spring, Angie had a moment to pause on the doorstep of the store, broom in hand, and admire the delicate blue of the sky. The gauzy clouds racing by almost looked like lace, and she daydreamed just for a moment about an elegant dress, just that color, trimmed with fine handmade lace. When she looked back to the street, a movement caught her eye—a spotted dog, long and lean and powerfully muscled, was tearing down the street oblivious to the occasional car or truck, every stride stretching its legs to their fullest extent.

"What a pretty dog," she thought to herself. "I wonder where it's going." In the hours ahead, though, Angie would completely forget the momentary encounter with the white dog with black spots because the little Midwestern city was hit by the most powerful tornado ever recorded, and she had her hands full salvaging what she could from the wreckage of her husband's store.

Over the years, stories about Annie continued to build. Mrs. Butler saw a Dalmatian rushing down the street the day before the boiler in her building exploded. Otto Sternhouser saw a strange dog on the street one day and told his wife over supper— the next day his delivery truck went out of control and plunged through the guardrail on the Seventh Avenue bridge. Time and time again, the sight of the powerful, sleek dog coursing through the streets was the harbinger of disaster, whether for one family or many.

The city grew and changed. All the streets were paved now, and traffic was controlled by electronic boxes sending signals to drivers; the vehicles all moved swiftly, each one hermetically sealed with its occupants isolated behind glass, steel, and plastic. A chemical factory was built across the river. Big supermarkets sprang up on the outskirts, and the little stores of downtown were replaced by strips of shops bordered by parking lots.

Hardly anything remained of the little city that Annie had known so well. Only the more substantial buildings still stood downtown—the two-, three-, and four-story structures of brick or stone. But even these were changed with new facades or garish signs covering the careful craftsmanship of builders long dead.

Still Annie was seen, and her presence reported. A local columnist even spent her week's allotment of words on the ghost dog that predicted disaster. But Mary Bolen prided herself on being practical, and she secretly scoffed at these stories.

"People should find better things to do than repeat such old wives' tales," she thought as she washed the dishes after a neighbor's visit. She didn't know it, but in a box in her attic was an old rag doll that still smelled strongly of smoke and whose smiling hand-stitched face was streaked with soot. It had belonged to her great-great-great-grandmother.

Mary had three children. Scott, the oldest, would be five soon, and she needed to buy party favors for his party coming up two weeks from Saturday. On a sunny Thursday afternoon, when the baby woke from her nap, Mary shepherded Scott and Andy, who was three, down the stairs and out to the car.

"Mama heard about a wonderful store," she explained to them, the baby squirming in her arms. "They have all kinds of neat toys and candy and stuff for parties!"

"Goo," said the baby sleepily.

"I wanna sit in the front seat," whined Andy. "How come Scotty always gets to sit in the front seat?"

"I'm bigger," Scott announced breezily, easily pushing Andy aside. Andy began to howl, and the baby started tuning up in sympathy.

Mary chewed the inside of her cheek for just a moment. "Scotty, I need you to help me with the baby," she said brightly. "Will you climb back here and get her buckled up?"

He looked at her suspiciously. "I wanna sit in the front seat," he complained. "You'll sit in the front seat on the way home," Mary ordered. "We take turns, and Mama gets to decide."

Andy stuck out his tongue at Scott. Mary ignored it and got all three children situated in their proper safety seats with the proper seat belts before releasing a very large sigh. Getting anywhere with three kids took an enormous amount of energy.

It didn't take long to get to the downtown area. Near the river, where the oldest buildings still stood, Mary navigated her way to the address she'd scribbled on a scrap of paper. It was a wholesale candy and toy place, but they sold to individuals, too. All these old, somber brick buildings looked half empty now, some with windows boarded up and scrawny alley cats sunning themselves on the stoops. The area seemed to be mostly a warehouse district. Big trucks thundered past, and Mary could see where the traffic had torn up the asphalt to reveal the old brick road beneath. She found a parking place a few doors down, and pulled the car up to the curb.

"Here we are," she said cheerfully. Thankfully, the baby had gone back to sleep, and Scott and Andy had forgotten their spat and jumped out of the car, intrigued by the unfamiliar neighborhood. They were talking animatedly, but since they were safely on the sidewalk, Mary didn't pay much attention. She was occupied with getting the baby out of her car seat without waking her up.

Scott was pointing at something, and Andy was jumping up and down when Mary straightened up, with the baby cocooned safely against her shoulder. At the end of the block, a sleek, lean

Dalmatian was headed toward them, loping at a comfortable speed. It was this graceful creature who had captured the boys' attention. As Mary watched, admiring the dog's fluid, easy motion down the dead center of the road, her mind registered the rumbling noise of a big truck rounding the corner. In the split second it took to realize the danger to the dog, she pulled the boys to her to cover their eyes.

"Mama, make it stop!" Andy had seen the danger, and his trust in her abilities knew no bounds.

Mary couldn't tear her eyes away from the impending disaster. Just as the truck bore down on the unsuspecting creature, Mary winced in anticipation of the grinding, heartrending noise of the collision, and she closed her eyes momentarily. When she opened them, the truck was gone, and the dog was streaking down the block unharmed. Mary released the boys but still clutched the baby tightly.

"Mama!" Andy threw his arms around her leg, giving her a grateful squeeze. It took a moment for her to realize that he thought she'd saved the dog.

Mary felt distinctly queasy. She urged the children into the store, a dim, cavernous room with wooden floors filled with metal shelving stacked up to the ceiling with box after box of candy and trinkets. It was a treasure trove, a child's conception of heaven, and Mary watched, smiling, as Scott and Andy debated the relative worth of candy snot compared to little buckets of candy dirt and gummy worms. They made it out of the store just at four o'clock, thirty dollars poorer but enriched with the currency of childhood: car-shaped erasers, bright beads, long spaghetti-like strands of fluorescent-colored bubble gum, and fifteen miniature pails of candy dirt and worms.

Dinner was chaotic. The baby, refreshed from her long nap

and taking her cue from the boys, happily slung food in every direction when Mary turned her back. Scott and Andy were keyed up by the afternoon's expedition and vied for their father's attention in voices that quickly escalated into shouting. It was all the adults could manage to keep the two little boys seated. In their excitement, they kept springing up to demonstrate one point or another.

"The shelves were this high, Daddy!" Scott rolled out of his chair and jumped, his hand held up in the air to show how tall.

"And they went on and on and on until it was dark!" Andy, not to be outdone, flung his arms out wide, forgetting that his fork had just speared a couple of green beans. Seeing them fly across the room, the baby chuckled and picked up a carrot and flung it in the same direction.

"And there was this dog, and Mama saved it!" This melodramatic pronouncement caused a momentary lull in the conversation.

John looked at his wife and raised his eyebrows. She just shook her head and smiled faintly before getting up to retrieve the green beans and the carrot. Remembering the incident made her feel queasy all over again.

Working swiftly and efficiently, the adults got each child cleaned up, tucked into pajamas, and situated in a bed or a crib. John read a story to the boys, stretched out between them on Andy's narrow bed, while Mary headed to the kitchen to start on the dishes. When her husband joined her, she was unusually quiet.

"What's wrong, honey?" John's voice was muffled—he'd thrust his head inside the cabinet to try to make room for the plastic salad bowl.

"I don't believe in ghosts."

"Ow." John came up, rubbing his head, and hastily shut the

cabinet door before all the bowls came rolling back out again. "I know you don't."

"But that dog was really strange."

"You think it was that dog the columnist wrote about—the disaster ghost dog?"

Mary forced herself to laugh. "Of course not!" She threw the sodden dish towel at her husband's head.

When the lights were out and John was just rolling over to get to sleep, she prodded him with her forefinger. "John," she whispered. "I just remembered. Beth called and wants to know if we can come up this weekend. Is that okay?"

"Sure, honey," he muttered sleepily.

"Right after work tomorrow, okay?"

"Okay, okay. Did you set the alarm clock?" His last sentence dissolved into a snore. It was hours later before Mary could compose her mind enough for sleep.

Mary packed the car and had the children waiting when her husband came home from work. As they passed the city limit sign, on their way north to see her sister, it was as if an invisible burden had lifted from her shoulders. She breathed easier.

The children played well with their cousins, John enjoyed the company of Beth's husband, and Mary and her sister reveled in the domestic peace—each feeling blessed by their healthy, happy family. That sense of satisfaction, bordering on smugness, made the shock even more appalling when Mary saw the familiar lines of her hometown on the Sunday morning TV news broadcast.

"Explosion at the chemical factory..." said the reporter, and Mary's legs gave out. She sank to the floor.

"Families evacuated..." the reporter droned on. Mary's mind was processing only bits and pieces of the horrible newscast.

"Spokesperson for the company declined to comment," the

reporter concluded, speaking over pictures of panic-stricken families throwing their belongings feverishly into their cars. "And in other news..."

A Fire-Fighter's Dog
Arthur Quiller-Couch

This is the story of a very distinguished member of the London Fire Brigade—the dog Chance. It proves that the fascinations of fires (and who that has witnessed a fire cannot own this fascination?) extends even to the brute creation. In old Egypt, Herodotus tells us, the cats used on the occasion of a conflagration to rush forth from their burning homes, and then madly attempt to return again; and the Egyptians, who worshiped the animals, had to form a ring round to prevent their dashing past and sacrificing themselves to the flames. This may, however, be due to the cat's notorious love for home. In the case of the dog Chance another hypothesis has to be searched for.

The animal formed his first acquaintance with the brigade by following a fireman from a conflagration in Shoreditch to the central station at Watling Street. Here, after he had been petted for some time by the men, his master came for him and took him home. But the dog quickly escaped and returned to the central station on the very first opportunity. He was carried back, returned, was carried back again, and again returned.

At this point his master—"like a mother whose son *will* go to sea"—abandoned the struggle and allowed him to follow his own course. Henceforth for years he invariably went with the engine, sometimes upon the carriage itself, sometimes under the horses' legs; and always, when going uphill, running in advance, and announcing by his bark the welcome news that the fire-engine was at hand.

Arrived at the fire, he would amuse himself with pulling burning logs of wood out of the flames with his mouth, firmly impressed that he was rendering the greatest service, and clearly anxious to show the laymen that he understood all about the business. Although he had his legs broken half a dozen times, he remained faithful to the profession he had so obstinately chosen. At last, having taken a more serious hurt than usual, he was being nursed by the firemen beside the hearth, when a "call" came. At the well-known sound of the engine turning out, the poor old dog made a last effort to climb upon it, and fell back—dead.

He was stuffed, and preserved at the station for some time. But even in death he was destined to prove the friend of the brigade. For, one of the engineers having committed suicide, the firemen determined to raffle him for the benefit of the widow, and such was his fame that he realized 123 pounds, 10 shillings, 9 pence, or over $615 in American money!

The Dog
Francis C. Woodworth

Whatever may be thought of the somewhat aristocratic pretensions of the lion, as the dog, after all, has the reputation of being the most intelligent of the inferior animals, I will allow this interesting family the precedence in these stories, and introduce them first to the reader. For the same reason, too—because they exhibit such wonderful marks of intelligence, approaching, sometimes, almost to the boundary of human reason—I shall occupy much more time in relating stories about them than about any other animal. Let me see. Where shall I begin? With Rover, my old friend Rover—my companion and play-fellow, when a little boy? I have a good mind to do so; for he endeared himself to me by thousands of acts of kindness and affection, and he has still a place of honor in my memory. He frequently went to school with me. As soon as he saw me get my satchel of books, he was at my side, and off he ran before me toward the school-house. When he had conducted me to school, he usually took leave of me, and returned home. But he came back again, before school was out, so as to be my companion homeward. I might tell a great many stories about the smartness of Rover; but on the whole I think I will forbear. I am afraid if I should talk half an hour about him, some of you would accuse me of too much partiality for my favorite, and would think I had fallen into the same foolish mistake that is sometimes noticed in over-fond fathers and mothers, who talk about a little boy or girl of theirs, as if there never was another such a prodigy. So I will just pass over Rover's wonderful exploits—for he had some, let me whisper it in your ear—and tell my stories about other people's dogs.

"Going to the dogs," is a favorite expression with a great many people. They understand by it a condition in the last degree deplorable. To "go to the dogs," is spoken of as being just about the worst thing that can happen to a poor fellow. I think differently, however. I wish from my heart, that some selfish persons whom I could name would go to the dogs. They would learn there, I am sure, what they have never learned before—most valuable lessons in gratitude, and affection, and self-sacrifice—to say nothing about common sense, a little more of which would not hurt them.

There is an exceedingly affecting story of a dog that lived in Scotland as long ago as 1716: This dog belonged to a Mr. Stewart, of Argyleshire, and was a great favorite with his master. He was a Highland greyhound, I believe. One afternoon, while his master was hunting in company with this dog, he was attacked with inflammation in his side. He returned home, and died the same evening. Some three days afterward his funeral took place, when the dog followed the remains of his master to the grave-yard, which was nearly ten miles from the residence of the family. He remained until the interment was completed, when he returned home with those who attended the funeral. When he entered the house he found the plaid cloak, formerly his master's, hanging in the entry. He pulled it down, and in defiance of all attempts to take it from him, lay on it all night, and would not even allow any person to touch it. Every evening afterward, about sunset, he left home, traveled to the grave-yard, reposed on the grave of his late master all night, and returned home regularly in the morning. But, what was still more remarkable, he could not be persuaded to eat a morsel. Children near the grave-yard, who watched his motions, again and again carried him food; but he resolutely refused it, and it was never known by what means he existed. While at home he was always dull and sorrowful; he usually lay in a sleeping posture, and frequently uttered long and mournful groans.

In the western part of our own country, some years since, an exploit was performed by a Newfoundland dog, which I must tell my readers. It is related by Mrs. Phelan. A man by the name of Wilson, residing near a river which was navigable, although the current was somewhat rapid, kept a pleasure boat. One day he invited a small party to accompany him in an excursion on the river. They set out. Among the number were Mr. Wilson's wife and little girl, about three years of age. The child was delighted with the boat, and with the water lilies that floated on the surface of the river. Meanwhile, a fine Newfoundland dog trotted along the bank of the stream, looking occasionally at the boat, and thinking, perhaps, that he should like a sail himself.

Pleasantly onward went the boat, and the party were in the highest spirits, when little Ellen, trying to get a pretty lily, stretched out her hand over the side of the boat, and in a moment she lost her balance and fell into the river. What language can describe the agony of those parents when they saw the current close over their dear child! The mother, in her terror, could hardly be prevented from throwing herself into the river to rescue her drowning girl, and her husband had to hold her back by force. Vain was the help of man at that dreadful moment; but prayer was offered up to God, and he heard it.

No one took any notice of Nero, the faithful dog. But he had kept his eye upon the boat, it seems. He saw all that was going on;

he plunged into the river at the critical moment when the child had sunk to the bottom, and dived beneath the surface. Suddenly a strange noise was heard on the side of the boat opposite to the one toward which the party were anxiously looking, and something seemed to be splashing in the water. It was the dog. Nero had dived to the bottom of that deep river, and found the very spot where the poor child had settled down into her cold, strange cradle of weeds and slime. Seizing her clothes, and holding them fast in his teeth, he brought her up to the surface of the water, a very little distance from the boat, and with looks that told his joy, he gave the little girl into the hands of her astonished father. Then, swimming back to the shore, he shook the water from his long, shaggy coat, and laid himself down, panting, to recover from the fatigue of his adventure.

Ellen seemed for awhile to be dead; her face was deadly pale; it hung on her shoulder; her dress showed that she had sunk to the bottom. But by and by she recovered gradually, and in less than a week she was as well as ever.

But the Glasgow Chronicle tells a story of the most supremely humane dog I ever heard of—so humane, in fact, that his humanity was somewhat troublesome. This dog—a fine Newfoundland—resided near Edinburgh.

Every day he was seen visiting all the ponds and brooks in the neighborhood of his master's residence. He had been instrumental more than once in saving persons from drowning. He was respected for his magnanimity, and caressed for his amiable qualities, till, strange as it may be considered, this flattery completely turned his head. Saving life became a passion. He took to it as men take to dram-drinking. Not having sufficient scope for the exercise of his diseased benevolence in the district, he took to a very questionable method of supplying the deficiency. Whenever he found a child on the brink of a pond, he watched patiently for the opportunity to place his fore-paws suddenly on its person, and plunged it in before it was aware. Now all this was done for the mere purpose of fetching them out again. He appeared to find intense pleasure in this nonsensical sort of work. At last the outcry became so great by parents alarmed for their children, although no life was ever lost by the indulgence of such a singular taste, that the poor dog was reluctantly destroyed.

Mr. Bingley, an English writer, has contributed not a little to the amusement and instruction of the young, by a book which he published a few years ago, relating to the instinct of the dog. Among the stories told in this book, are several which I must transfer for my own readers. Here is one about the fatal adventure of a large mastiff with a robber. I shall give it nearly in the words of Mr. Bingley.

Not a great many years ago, a lady, who resided in a lonely house in Cheshire, England, permitted all her domestics, save one female, to go to a supper at an inn about three miles distant, which was kept by the uncle of the girl who remained at home with her mistress. As the servants were not expected to return till the morning, all the doors and windows were as usual secured, and the lady and her companion were about to retire to bed, when they were alarmed by the noise of some persons apparently attempting to break into the house. A large mastiff, which fortunately happened to be in the kitchen, set up a tremendous barking; but this had not the effect of intimidating the robbers.

After listening attentively for some time, the maid-servant discovered that the robbers were attempting to enter the house by forcing their way through a hole under the sunk story in the back kitchen. Being a young woman of courage, she went toward the spot, accompanied by the dog, and patting him on the back, exclaimed, "At him, Caesar!" The dog leaped into the hole, made a furious attack upon the intruder, and gave something a violent shake. In a few minutes all became quiet, and the animal returned with his mouth full of blood. A slight bustle was now heard outside the house, but in a short time all again became still. The lady and servant, too much terrified to think of going to bed, sat up until morning without further molestation. When day dawned they discovered a quantity of blood outside of the wall in the court-yard.

When her fellow-servants came home, they brought word to the girl that her uncle, the inn-keeper, had died suddenly of apoplexy during the night, and that it was intended that the funeral should take place in the course of the day. Having obtained leave to go to the funeral, she was surprised to learn, on her arrival, that the coffin was screwed down. She insisted, however, on taking a last look at the body, which was most unwillingly granted; when, to her great surprise and horror, she discovered that his death had been occasioned by a large wound in the throat. The events of the preceding night rushed on her mind, and it soon became evident to her that she had been the innocent and unwilling cause of her uncle's death. It turned out, that he and one of his servants had formed the design of robbing the house and murdering the lady during the absence of her servants, but that their wicked design had been frustrated by the courage and watchfulness of her faithful mastiff.

There is another anecdote told of a wild Indian dog which I am sure my young friends will like. It is from the same source with the one about the mastiff. A man by the name of Le Fevre, many years ago, lived on a farm in the United States, near the Blue mountains. Those mountains at that time abounded in deer and other animals. One day, the youngest of Le Fevre's children, who was four years old, disappeared early in the morning. The family, after a partial search, becoming alarmed, had recourse to the assistance of some

The Dog

neighbors. These separated into parties, and explored the woods in every direction, but without success. Next day the search was renewed, but with no better result. In the midst of their distress Tewenissa, a native Indian from Anaguaga, on the eastern branch of the river Susquehannah, who happened to be journeying in that quarter, accompanied by his dog Oniah, happily went into the house of the planter with the design of reposing himself. Observing the distress of the family, and being informed of the circumstances, he requested that the shoes and stockings last worn by the child should be brought to him. He then ordered his dog to smell them; and taking the house for a centre, described a semicircle of a quarter of a mile, urging the dog to find out the scent. They had not gone far before the sagacious animal began to bark. The track was followed up by the dog with still louder barking, till at last, darting off at full speed, he was lost in the thickness of the woods. Half an hour after they saw him returning. His countenance was animated, bearing even an expression of joy; it was evident he had found the child—but was he dead or alive? This was a moment of cruel suspense, but it was of short continuance. The Indian followed his dog, and the excellent animal conducted him to the lost child, who was found unharmed, lying at the foot of a great tree. Tewenissa took him in his arms, and returned with him to the distressed parents and their friends, who had not been able to advance with the same speed. He restored little Derick to his father and mother, who ran to meet him; when a scene of tenderness and gratitude ensued, which may be easier felt than described. The child was in a state of extreme weakness, but, by means of a little care, he was in a short time restored to his usual vigor.

In one of the churches at Lambeth, England, there is a painting on a window, representing a man with his dog. There is a story connected with this painting which is worth telling. Tradition

169

informs us that a piece of ground near Westminster bridge, containing a little over an acre, was left to that parish by a pedler, upon condition that his picture, accompanied by his dog, should be faithfully painted on the glass of one of the windows. The parishioners, as the story goes, had this picture executed accordingly, and came in possession of the land. This was in the year 1504. The property rented at that time for about a dollar a year. It now commands a rent of nearly fifteen hundred dollars. The reason given for the pedler's request is, that he was once very poor, when, one day, having occasion to pass across this piece of ground, and being weary, he sat down under a tree to rest. While seated here, he noticed that his dog, who was with him, acted strangely. At a distance of several rods from the place where he sat, the dog busied himself for awhile in scratching at a particular spot of earth, after which he returned to his master, looked earnestly up to his face, and endeavored to draw him toward the spot where he had been digging. The pedler, however, paid but little attention to the movements of the dog, until he had repeated them several times, when he was induced to accompany the dog. To his surprise he found, on doing so, that there was a pot of gold buried there. With a part of this gold he purchased the lot of ground on which it had been discovered, and bequeathed it to the parish on the conditions mentioned above. The pedler and his dog are represented in the picture which ornaments the window of that church. "But is the story a true one?" methinks I hear my little friends inquire. I confess it has the air of one of Baron Munchausen's yarns, and I am somewhat doubtful about it. But that is the tradition in the Lambeth parish, where the picture may still be seen by any body who takes the trouble to visit the place. The story may be true. Stranger things have happened.

Those who have studied geography do not need to be informed that there is a chain of high mountains running through

Switzerland, called the Alps. The tops of some of these mountains are covered with snow nearly all the year. In the winter it is very difficult and dangerous traveling over the Alps; for the snow frequently rolls down the sides of the mountain, in a great mass, called an *avalanche*, and buries the traveler beneath it. On one of these mountains there is the convent of St. Bernard. It is situated ten thousand feet above the base of the mountain, and is on one of the most dangerous passes between Switzerland and Savoy. It is said to be the highest inhabited spot in the old world. It is tenanted by a race of monks, who are very kind to travelers. Among other good services they render to the strangers who pass near their convent, they search for unhappy persons who have been overtaken by sudden storms, and who are liable to perish.

These monks have a peculiar variety of the dog, called the dog of St. Bernard, or the Alpine Spaniel, which they train to hunt for travelers who are overtaken by a storm, and who are in danger of perishing. The dog of St. Bernard is one of the most sagacious of his species. He is covered with thick, curly hair, which is frequently of great service in warming the traveler, when he is almost dead with cold.

One of these dogs, named Barry, had, it was reckoned, in twelve years saved the lives of forty individuals. Whenever the mountain was enveloped in fogs and snow, away scoured Barry, barking and searching all about for any person who might have fallen a victim to the storm. When he was successful in finding any one, if his own strength was insufficient to rescue him, he would run back to the convent in search of assistance.

I think I must translate for my young readers an affecting story about this dog Barry, which I read the other day in a little French book, entitled "Modeles des Enfans." It seems that a great while ago there was a poor woman wandering about these mountains, in the vicinity of the convent of St. Bernard, in company with her son, a very small boy. The story does not inform us what they were doing, and why they were walking in such a dangerous place. Perhaps they were gathering fuel to keep them warm; and very likely when they left home the weather was mild, and that they did not anticipate a storm. However that may be, they were overtaken by an avalanche, the mother was buried beneath it, and the child saw her no more. But I must tell the remainder of the story in the language of the French writer.

"Poor boy! the storm increased; the wind howled, and whirled the snow into huge heaps. In the hope that he might possibly meet a traveler, the child forced his way for awhile through the snow; but at last, exhausted, benumbed with the cold, and discouraged, he fell upon his knees, joined his hands devoutly together, and cried, as he raised his face, bathed in tears, toward heaven, 'O my God! have mercy on a poor child, who has nobody in the world to care for him!' As he lay in the place where he fell down, which was sheltered a little by a rock, he grew colder and colder, and he thought he must die. But still, from time to time, he prayed, 'Have mercy, O my God! on a poor child, who has nobody in the world to care for him!' At last he fell asleep, but was wakened by feeling a warm paw on his face. As he opened his eyes he saw with terror an enormous dog holding his head near his own. He uttered a cry of fear, and started back a little way from the dog. The dog approached the boy again, and tried, after his own fashion, to make the little fellow understand that he came there to do him good, and not to hurt him. Then he licked the face and hands of the child. By and by the child confided in his visitor, and began to entertain a hope that he might yet be saved. When Barry saw that his errand was understood, he lifted his head, and showed the child a bottle covered with willow, which was hanging around his neck. This bottle contained wine, some of which the little fellow drank, and felt refreshed. Then the dog lay down by the side of the child, and gave him the benefit of the heat of his own body for a long time. After this, the dog made a sign for the boy to get upon his back. It was some time before the boy could understand what the sign meant. But it was repeated again and again, and at last the child mounted the back of the kind animal, who carried him safely to the convent."

Here is a capital story about a bloodhound, taken from the excellent book by Mr. Bingley, to which I have before alluded. Aubri de Mondidier, a gentleman of family and fortune, traveling alone through the Forest of Bondy, in France, was murdered, and buried under a tree. His dog, a bloodhound, would not quit his master's grave for several days; till at length, compelled by hunger, he proceeded to the house of an intimate friend of the unfortunate Aubri at Paris, and, by his melancholy howling, seemed desirous of expressing the loss they had both sustained. He repeated his cries, ran to the door, looked back to see if any one followed him, returned to his master's friend, pulled him by the sleeve, and with dumb eloquence, entreated him to go with him. The singularity of all these actions of the dog, added to the circumstance of his coming there without his master, whose faithful companion he had always been, prompted the company to follow the animal. He conducted them to the foot of a tree, where he renewed his howling, scratching the earth with his feet, and significantly entreating them to search the particular spot. Accordingly, on digging, the body of the unhappy Aubri was found.

Some time after, the dog accidentally met the assassin, who is styled, by all the historians who relate the story, the Chevalier Macaire, when, instantly seizing him by the throat, he was with great difficulty compelled to quit his victim. In short, whenever the dog saw the chevalier, he continued to pursue and attack him with equal fury. Such obstinate violence, confined only to Macaire, appeared very extraordinary, especially to those who at once recalled the dog's remarkable attachment to his master, and several instances in which Macaire's envy and hatred to Aubri de Mondidier had been conspicuous.

Additional circumstances increased suspicion, and at length the affair reached the royal ear. The king accordingly sent for the dog, which appeared extremely gentle, till he perceived Macaire in the midst of several noblemen, when he ran fiercely toward him, growling at and attacking him, as usual. Struck with such a combination of circumstantial evidence against Macaire, the king determined to refer the decision to the chance of battle; or, in other words, he gave orders for a combat between the chevalier and the dog. The lists were appointed in the Isle of Notre Dame, then an unenclosed, uninhabited place. Macaire was allowed for his weapon a great cudgel, and an empty cask was given to the dog as a place of retreat, to enable him to recover breath.

Every thing being prepared, the dog no sooner found himself at liberty, than he made for his adversary, running round him and menacing him on every side, avoiding his blows till his strength was exhausted; then springing forward, he seized him by the throat, threw him on the ground, and obliged him to confess his guilt in presence of the king and the whole court. In consequence of this confession, the chevalier, after a few days, was convicted upon his own acknowledgment, and beheaded on a scaffold in the Isle of Notre Dame.

The editor of the Portland (Maine) Advertiser relates the following anecdote: "A gentleman from the country recently drove up to a store in this city, and jumping from his sleigh, left his dog in the care of the vehicle. Presently an avalanche of snow slid from the top of the building upon the sidewalk, which so frightened the horse that he started off down the street at a furious run. At this critical juncture, the dog sprang from the sleigh, and seizing the reins in his mouth, held back with all his strength, and actually reined in the frightened animal to a post at the side of the street, when apparently having satisfied himself that no danger was to be apprehended, he again resumed his station in the sleigh, as unconcerned as if he had only done an ordinary act of duty."

A few years ago a little girl, residing in an inland village in Connecticut—without the consent of her mother, be it remembered—went alone to a pond near by, to play with her brother's little vessel, and fell into the water. She came very near drowning; but a dog belonging to the family, named Rollo, who was not far off, plunged in and drew her to the shore. She was so exhausted, however, that she could not rise, and the dog could not lift her entirely out of the water. But he raised her head a little above the surface, and then ran after help. He found a man, and made use of every expedient in his power to draw him to the spot where he had left the child. At first the stranger paid very little attention to the dog; but by and by he was persuaded something was wrong, and followed the dog to the pond. The little girl was not drowned, though she was quite insensible; and the man lifted her from the water, and saved her life, to the great joy of Rollo, who seemed eager to assist in this enterprise.

Here is a capital story about a shepherd's dog in Scotland. I take the liberty of borrowing it from Bingley's admirable book. The valleys, or glens, as they are called by the natives, which intersect the Grampians, a ridge of rocky and precipitous mountains in the northern part of Scotland, are chiefly inhabited by shepherds. As the pastures over which each flock is permitted to range, extend many miles in every direction, the shepherd never has a view of his whole flock at once, except when it is collected for the purpose of sale or shearing. His occupation is to make daily visits to the different extremities of his pastures in succession, and to turn back, by means of his dog, any stragglers that may be approaching the boundaries of his neighbors.

In one of these excursions, a shepherd happened to carry with him one of his children, an infant some two or three years old. After traversing his pastures for some time, attended by his dog, the shepherd found himself under the necessity of ascending a summit at some distance to have a more extended view of his range. As the ascent was too fatiguing for his child, he left him on a small plain at the bottom, with strict injunctions not to stir from it till his return. Scarcely, however, had he gained the summit, when the horizon was suddenly darkened by one of those thick and heavy fogs which frequently descend so rapidly amid these mountains, as, in the space of a few minutes, almost to turn day into night. The anxious father instantly hastened back to find his child; but, owing to the unusual darkness, and his own trepidation, he unfortunately missed his way in the descent. After a fruitless search of many hours among the dangerous morasses and cataracts with which these mountains abound, he was at length overtaken by night. Still wandering on, without knowing whither, he at length came to the verge of the mist, and, by the light of the moon, discovered that he had reached the bottom of the valley, and was now within a short distance of his cottage. To renew the search that night was equally fruitless and dangerous. He was therefore obliged to return home, having lost both his child and his dog, which had attended him faithfully for years.

Next morning by day-break, the shepherd, accompanied by a band of his neighbors, set out again to seek his child; but, after a day spent in fruitless fatigue, he was at last compelled by the approach of night to descend from the mountain. On returning to his cottage, he found that the dog which he had lost the day before, had been home, and, on receiving a piece of cake, had instantly gone off again. For several successive days the shepherd renewed the search for his child, and still, on returning in the evening disappointed to his cottage, he found that the dog had been there, and, on receiving his usual allowance of cake, had instantly disappeared. Struck with this singular circumstance, he remained at home one day, and when the dog, as usual, departed with his piece of cake, he resolved to follow him, and find out the cause of this strange procedure. The dog led the way to a cataract at some distance from the spot where the shepherd had left his child. The banks of the waterfall, almost joined at the top, yet separated by an abyss of immense depth, presented that abrupt appearance which so often astonishes and appalls the traveler amid the Grampian mountains, and indicates that these stupendous chasms were not the silent work of time, but the sudden effect of some violent convulsion of the earth. Down one of these rugged and almost perpendicular descents the dog began, without hesitation, to make his way, and at last disappeared in a cave, the mouth of which was almost on a level with the torrent. The shepherd with difficulty followed; but, on entering the cave, what were his emotions, when he beheld his infant eating with much satisfaction the cake which the dog had just brought him, while the faithful animal stood by, eyeing his young charge with the utmost complacency! From the situation in which the child was found, it appeared that he had wandered to the brink of the precipice, and either fallen or scrambled down till he reached the cave, which the dread of the torrent had afterward prevented him from quitting. The dog, by means of his scent, had traced him to the spot, and afterward prevented him from starving, by giving up to him his own daily allowance. He appears never to have quitted the child by night or day, except when it was necessary to go for his food, and then he was always seen running at full speed to and from the cottage.

The following story is related on the authority of a correspondent of the Boston Traveler: A gentleman from abroad, stopping at a hotel in Boston, privately secreted his handkerchief behind the cushion of a sofa, and left the hotel, in company with his dog. After walking for some minutes, he suddenly stopped, and said to his dog, "I have left my handkerchief at the hotel, and want it"—giving no particular directions in reference to it. The dog immediately returned in full speed, and entered the room which his master had just left. He went directly to the sofa, but the handkerchief was gone. He jumped upon tables and counters, but it was not to be seen. It proved that a friend had discovered it, and supposing that it had been left by mistake, had retained it for the owner. But Tiger was not to be foiled. He flew about the room, apparently much excited, in quest of the "lost or stolen." Soon, however, he was upon the track; he scented it to the gentleman's coat pocket. What was to be done? The dog had no means of asking verbally for it, and was not accustomed to picking pockets; and, besides, the gentleman was ignorant of his business with him. But Tiger's sagacity did not suffer him to remain long in suspense; he seized the skirt containing the prize, and furiously tore it from the coat, and hastily made off with it, much to the surprise of its owner. Tiger overtook his master, and restored the lost property, receiving his approbation, notwithstanding he did it at the expense of the gentleman's coat. At a subsequent interview, the gentleman refused any remuneration for his torn garment, declaring that the joke was worth the price of his coat.

One day, as a little girl was amusing herself with a child, near Carlisle Bridge, Dublin, and was sportively toying with the child, he made a sudden spring from her arms, and in an instant fell into the river. The screaming nurse and anxious spectators saw the water close over the child, and conceived that he had sunk to rise no more. A Newfoundland dog, which had been accidentally passing with his master, sprang forward to the wall, and gazed wistfully at the ripple in the water, made by the child's descent. At the same instant the dog sprang forward to the edge of the water. While the animal was descending, the child again sunk, and the faithful creature was seen anxiously swimming round and round the spot where he had disappeared. Once more the child rose to the surface; the dog seized him, and with a firm but gentle pressure, bore him to land without injury. Meanwhile a gentleman arrived, who, on inquiry into the circumstances of the transaction, exhibited strong marks of interest and feeling toward the child, and of admiration for the dog that had rescued him from death. The person who had removed the child from the dog turned to show him to the gentleman, when there were presented to his view the well-known features of his own son! A mixed sensation of terror, joy, and surprise, struck him mute. When he had recovered the use of his faculties, and fondly kissed his little darling, he lavished a thousand embraces on the dog, and offered to his master five hundred guineas if he would transfer the valuable animal to him; but the owner of the dog felt too much affection for the useful creature, to part with him for any consideration whatever.

A boatman on the river Thames, in England, once laid a wager that he and his dog would leap from the centre arch of Westminster Bridge, and land at Lambeth within a minute of each other. He jumped off first, and the dog immediately followed; but as he was not in the secret, and fearing that his master would be drowned, he seized him by the neck, and dragged him on shore, to the great diversion of the spectators.

Some years ago, a gentleman of Queen's College, Oxford, went to pass the Christmas vacation at his father's in the country. An uncle, a brother, and other friends, were one day to dine together. It was fine, frosty weather; the two young gentlemen went out for a forenoon's recreation, and one of them took his skates with him. They were followed by a favorite greyhound. When the friends were beginning to long for their return, the dog came home at full speed, and by his apparent anxiety, his laying hold of their clothes to pull them along, and all his gestures, he convinced them that something was wrong. They followed the greyhound, who led them to a piece of water frozen over. A hat was seen on the ice, near which was a fresh aperture. The bodies of the young gentlemen were soon found, but, alas! though every means were tried, life could not be restored.

There is another story which places the sagacity of the greyhound in still stronger light. A Scotch gentleman, who kept a greyhound and a pointer, being fond of coursing, employed the one to find the hares, and the other to catch them. It was, however, discovered, that when the season was over, the dogs were in the habit of going out by themselves, and killing hares for their own amusement. To prevent this, a large iron ring was fastened to the pointer's neck by a leather collar, and hung down so as to prevent the dog from running or jumping over dikes. The animals, however, continued to stroll out to the fields together; and one day, the gentleman suspecting that all was not right, resolved to watch them, and, to his surprise, found that the moment they thought they were unobserved, the greyhound took up the ring in his mouth, and carrying it, they set off to the hills, and began to search for hares, as usual. They were followed; and it was observed that whenever the pointer scented the hare, the ring was dropped, and the greyhound stood ready to pounce upon the game the moment the other drove her from her form; but that he uniformly returned to assist his companion, after he had caught his prey.

Some of the dogs belonging to the gipsies possess a great deal of shrewdness. The gipsies, you know, are a very singular race of people. They are scattered over a great portion of Europe, wandering from place to place, and living in miserable tents, or huts. You can form a pretty correct notion of a gipsy encampment, by the picture on another page. Here you see the gipsy men and women, sitting and standing around a fire, over which is a pot, evidently containing the material for their meal. If you notice the picture carefully, you will observe, also, a little, insignificant looking dog, who is apparently asleep, and, for aught I know, dreaming about the exploits of the day. You will no doubt smile, and wonder what exploits such a cur is able to perform; but I assure you that if he is at all like some of the gipsy dogs I have heard of, he has been taught a good many very shrewd tricks. The dogs of the gipsies are sometimes trained to steal for their masters. The thief enters a store with some respectably dressed man, whom the owner of the dog will commission for the purpose, and—the man having made certain signals to the animal—the gipsy cur, after loitering about the store, perhaps for hours, waiting a favorable opportunity, will steal the articles which were designated, and run away with them to his master's tent.

I made the acquaintance of a dog at Niagara Falls, last summer, who was an ardent admirer of the beautiful and grand in nature. The little steamer called the "Maid of the Mist" makes several trips daily, from a point some two miles down the river, to within a few rods of the Canada Fall. I went up in this boat, one morning, and the trip afforded me one of the finest views I had of this inimitable cataract. Among the passengers in this boat, at the time, was the dog who was so fond of the sublime. He walked leisurely on board, just before the hour of starting, and during the entire excursion seemed to enjoy the scene as much as any of the rest of the passengers. As the boat approached the American Fall, he took his station in the bow, where he remained, completely deluged in the spray, until the boat passed the same Fall, on its return. This, however, is not the most remarkable part of the story. The captain informed me that such was the daily practice of the dog. Every morning, regularly, at the hour of starting, he makes his appearance, though he is not owned by any one engaged in the boat, and treats himself to this novel excursion.

There is a dog living on Staten Island, who has for some time been acting the part of a philanthropist, on a large scale. He makes it a great share of his business to administer to the necessities of the sick and infirm dogs in the neighborhood. As soon as he learns that a dog is sick, so that he is unable to take care of himself, he visits the invalid, and nurses him; and he even goes from house to house, searching out those who need his assistance. Frequently he brings his patient to his own kennel, and takes care of him until he either gets well or dies. Sometimes he has two or three sick dogs in his hospital, at the same time. I have these facts on the authority of my friend Mr. Ranlett, the editor of the "Architect," a gentleman of unquestionable veracity, who has seen the dog thus imitating the example of the Good Samaritan.

Captain Parry, an adventurous sailor, who went out from England on a voyage of discovery in the northern seas, relates some amusing anecdotes about the dogs among the Esquimaux Indians. These dogs are trained to draw a vehicle called a sledge, made a little like what we call a sleigh. In some parts of Russia many people travel in the same manner. Here is a picture of one of the Russian sledges. It is made in very handsome style, as you see. The greater portion of them are constructed much more rudely. The Esquimaux

The Dog

Indian is famous for his feats in driving dogs. When he wants to take a ride, he harnesses up several pairs of these dogs, and off he goes, almost as swift as the wind. The dogs are rather unruly, however, sometimes, and get themselves sadly snarled together, so that the driver is obliged to go through the harnessing process several times in the course of a drive of a few miles. When the road is level and pretty smoothly worn, eight or ten dogs, with a weight only of some six or seven hundred pounds attached to them, are almost unmanageable, and will run any where they choose at the rate of ten miles an hour.

The following anecdote we have on the authority of the *Newark (N.J.) Daily Advertiser*: An officer of the army, accompanied by his dog, left West Point on a visit to the city of Burlington, N. J., and while there, becoming sick, wrote to his wife and family at West Point, in relation to his indisposition. Shortly after the reception of his letter, the family were aroused by a whining, barking and scratching, at the door of the house, and when opened to ascertain the cause, in rushed the faithful dog. After being caressed, and every attempt made to quiet him, the dog, in despair at not being understood, seized a shawl in his teeth, and, placing his paws on the lady's shoulders, deposited there the shawl! He then placed himself before her, and, fixing his gaze intently upon her, to attract her attention, seized her dress, and began to drag her to the door. The lady then became alarmed, and sent for a relative, who endeavored to allay her fears, but she prevailed upon him to accompany her at once to her husband, and on arriving, found him dangerously ill in Burlington. The distance traveled by the faithful animal, and the difficulties encountered, render this exploit almost incredible, especially as the boats could not stop at West Point, on account of the ice, it being in the winter.

There is a dog in the city of New York, who, according to unquestionable authority, is accustomed every day not only to bring his mistress the morning paper, as soon as it is thrown into the front yard, but to select the one belonging to the lady, when, as is frequently the case, there is one lying with it belonging to another member of the family.

An unfortunate dog, living in England, in order to make sport for some fools, had a pan tied to his tail, and was sent off on his travels toward a village a few miles distant. He reached the place utterly exhausted, and lay down before the steps of a tavern, eyeing most anxiously the horrid annoyance hung behind him, but unable to move a step further, or rid himself of the torment. Another dog, a Scotch colly, came up at the time, and seeing the distress of his crony, laid himself down gently beside him, and gaining his confidence by a few caresses, proceeded to gnaw the string by which the noisy appendage was attached to his friend's tail, and by about a quarter of an hour's exertion, severed the cord, and started to his legs, with the pan hanging from the string in his mouth, and after a few joyful capers around his friend, departed on his travels, in the highest glee at his success.

The Albany Journal tells us of a dog in that city, who has formed the habit of regarding a shadow with a great deal of interest. In this particular, he is not unlike some people that one occasionally meets with, who spend their whole time following shadows. The story of the Albany editor is thus told: Those who are in the habit of frequenting the post-office, between the hours of six and eight in the evening, have doubtless noticed the singular wanderings of a dog near the first swing door, without knowing the cause of his mysterious actions. The hall is lighted with gas, and the burner is placed between the two doors. When the outer door swings, the frame-work of the sash throws a moving shadow on the wall, beneath the structure, which, from its peculiar movement toward the floor, has attracted the notice of this dog. He watches it as sharp as if it were a mouse, and although his labors have been fruitless, yet he still continues nightly to grace this place with his presence. Several attempts have been made to draw his attention from the object, with but little success; for though his attention may be diverted, it is soon lost, as the instant his eye catches the shadow, he renews his watchings. In all his movements he is very harmless, and he neither injures nor even molests those who have occasion to pass through the hall.

As a farmer of good circumstances, who resided in the county of Norfolk, England, was taking an excursion to a considerable distance from home, during the frosts in the month of March 1795, he at length was so benumbed by the intense cold, that he became stupefied, and so sleepy that he found himself unable to proceed. He lay down, and would have perished on the spot, had not a faithful dog, which attended him, as if sensible of his dangerous situation, got on his breast, and, extending himself over him, preserved the circulation of his blood. The dog, so situated for many hours, kept up a continual barking, by which means, and the assistance of some passengers, the farmer was roused, and led to a house, where he soon recovered.

Carlo, the Soldiers' Dog
General Rush C. Hawkins

The Ninth New York Volunteers was organized in April 1861, in the City of New York. Two of the companies were made up of men from outside the city. C was composed of men from Hoboken and Paterson, New Jersey, and G marched into the regimental headquarters fully organized from the town of Fort Lee in that State. With this last named company came Carlo, the subject of this sketch.

When he joined the regiment, he had passed beyond the period of puppyhood and was in the full flush of dogly beauty. He was large, not very large,—would probably have turned the scales at about fifty pounds. His build was decidedly "stocky," and, as horsey men would say, his feet were well under him; his chest was broad and full, back straight, color a warm dark brindle, nose and lips very black, while he had a broad, full forehead and a wonderful pair of large, round, soft, dark-brown eyes. Add to this description an air of supreme, well-bred dignity, and you have an idea of one of the noblest animals that ever lived.

His origin was obscure; one camp reunion asserted that he was born on board of a merchant ship while his mother was making a passage from Calcutta to New York; and another told of a beautiful mastiff living somewhere in the State of New Jersey that had the honor of bringing him into the world. It would be very interesting to know something of the parentage of our hero, but since the facts surrounding his birth are unattainable, we must content ourselves with telling a portion of a simple story of a good and noble life. It may be safe to assert that he was not a native American; if he had been, he would have provided himself with the regulation genealogical tree and family coat-of-arms.

During the first part of his term of service, Carlo was very loyal to his company, marched, messed, and slept with it; but he was not above picking up, here and there, from the mess tents of the other companies a tid-bit, now and then, which proved acceptable to a well-appointed digestion.

His first turn on guard was performed as a member of the detail from Co. G, and always afterward, in the performance of that duty, he was most faithful. No matter who else might be late, he was ever on time when the call for guard mount was sounded, ready to go out with his own particular squad. At first, he would march back to company quarters with the old detail, but, as soon as he came to realize the value and importance of guard duty, he made up his mind that his place was at the guard tent and on the patrol beat, where he could be of the greatest service in watching the movements of the enemy.

In the performance of his duties as a member of the guard he was very conscientious and ever on the alert. No stray pig, wandering sheep, or silly calf could pass in front of his part of the line without being investigated by him. It is possible that his vigilance in investigating intruding meats was sharpened by the hope of substantial recognition in the way of a stray rib extracted from the marauding offender whose ignorance of army customs in time of war had brought it too near our lines.

As a rule, Carlo, what with his guard duties and other purely

Carlo, the Soldier's Dog

routine items, managed to dispose of the day until dress parade. At that time he appeared at his best, and became the regimental dog.

No officer or soldier connected with the command more fully appreciated "The pomp and circumstance of great and glorious war" than he. As the band marched out to take position previous to playing for the companies to assemble, he would place himself alongside the drum-major, and, when the signal for marching was given, would move off with stately and solemn tread, with head well up, looking straight to the front. Upon those great occasions, he fully realized the dignity of his position, and woe betide any unhappy other dog that happened to get in front of the marching band. When upon the parade field, he became, next to the colonel, the commanding officer, and ever regarded himself as the regulator of the conduct of those careless and frivolous dogs, that go about the world like street urchins, having no character for respectability or position in society to sustain.

Of those careless ne'er-do-wells the company had accumulated a very large following. As a rule, they were harmless and companionable, and were always on hand ready for a free lunch. It was only on dress parade that they made themselves over-officious. Each company was attended to the parade ground by its particular family of canine companions, and, when all of them had assembled, the second battalion of the regiment would make itself known by a great variety of jumpings, caperings, barks of joy, and cries of delight. To this unseasonable hilarity Carlo seriously objected, and his actions plainly told the story of his disgust at the conduct of the silly members of his race. He usually remained a passive observer until the exercise in the manual of arms, at which particular period in the ceremonies, the caperings and the barkings would become quite unendurable. Our hero would then assume the character of a preserver of the peace. He would make for the nearest group of

189

revellers, and, in as many seconds, give a half dozen or more of them vigorous shakes, which would set them to howling, and warn the others of the thoughtless tribe of an impending danger. Immediately the offenders would all scamper to another part of the field, and remain quiet until the dress parade was over. This duty was self-imposed and faithfully performed upon many occasions.

After the parade was dismissed Carlo would march back to quarters with his own company, where he would remain until the last daily distributions of rations, whereupon, after having disposed of his share, he would start out upon a tour of regimental inspection, making friendly calls at various company quarters and by taps turning up at the headquarters of the guard. His duties ended for the day, he would enjoy his well-earned rest until reveille, unless some event of an unusual nature, occurring during the night, disturbed his repose and demanded his attention.

During the first year of his service in the field, Carlo was very fortunate. He had shared in all the transportations by water, in all the marchings, skirmishes, and battles, without receiving a scratch or having a day's illness. But his good fortune was soon to end, for it was ordained that, like other brave defenders, he was to suffer in the great cause for which all were risking their lives.

The morning of April 18, 1862, my brigade, then stationed at Roanoke Island, embarked upon the steamer *Ocean Wave* for an expedition up the Elizabeth River, the object of which was to destroy the locks of the Dismal Swamp canal in order to prevent several imaginary iron-clads from getting into Albemarle Sound.

Among the first to embark was the ever ready and faithful Carlo, and the next morning, when his companions disembarked near Elizabeth City, he was one of the first to land, and, during the whole of the long and dreary march of thirty miles to Camden Court House, lasting from three o'clock in the morning until one in the afternoon, he was ever on the alert, but keeping close to his regiment. The field of battle was reached; the engagement, in which his command met with a great loss, commenced and ended, and, when the particulars of the disaster were inventoried, it was ascertained that a Confederate bullet had taken the rudimentary claw from Carlo's left fore-leg. This was his first wound, and he bore it like a hero without a whine or even a limp. A private of Co. G, who first noticed the wound, exclaimed: "Ah, Carlo, what a pity you are not an officer! If you were, the loss of that claw would give you sixty days' leave and a brigadier general's commission at the end of it." That was about the time that generals' commissions had become very plentiful in the Department of North Carolina.

The command re-embarked, and reached Roanoke Island the morning after the engagement, in time for the regulation "Hospital or Sick Call," which that day brought together an unusual number of patients, and among them Carlo, who was asked to join the waiting line by one of the wounded men. When his turn came to be inspected by the attending surgeon, he was told to hold up the wounded leg, which he readily did, and then followed the washing, the application of simple cerate, and the bandaging, with a considerable show of interest and probable satisfaction.

Thereafter, there was no occasion to ask him to attend the surgeon's inspection. Each morning, as soon as the bugle call was sounded, he would take his place in line with the other patients, advance in his turn, and receive the usual treatment. This habit continued until the wound was healed.

Always, after this, to every friendly greeting, he would respond by holding up the wounded leg for inspection, and he acted as though he thought that everybody was interested in the honorable scar that told the story of patriotic duty faithfully performed.

Later on, for some reason known to himself, Carlo transferred his special allegiance to Co. K. and maintained close connection with that company until the end of his term of service. He was regarded by its members as a member of the company mess, and was treated as one of them. But, notwithstanding his special attachments, there can be no reasonable doubt about his having considered himself a member of the regiment, clothed with certain powers and responsibilities. At the end of his term he was fitted with a uniform—trousers, jacket, and fez, and, thus dressed, he marched up Broadway, immediately behind the band. He was soon after mustered out of the service, and received an honorable discharge, not signed with written characters, but attested by the good-will of every member of the regiment.